Intelligence

Intelligence

by Endru Atros

TABLE OF CONTENTS

PROLOGUE

(I'm not sure if this introduction is really a prologue?)

She left the party early, but for her, it was still very late. She had promised herself she would review her computer science notes in the morning. It wasn't that she didn't know the subject, but she was interested in expanding her knowledge. She wanted to know more than what was in the assigned material.

"Aga, I'm crashing. Have fun," she said to her cousin.

"Let me at least get you a taxi," Aga offered, unconvincingly. She knew Joanna wouldn't take any money from her. She never did, for the simple reason that she would have nothing to pay her back with. Sometimes Aga would hail a cab for her and pay the driver in advance, pretending she was going home, too. After a while, she would change her mind and get out under some pretext. Then Joasia would continue on alone.

Tonight, Joanna hadn't wanted to go outside. To this day, she terribly regrets it.

Although Joanna wasn't far from the Metro station, it was already after midnight. It was dreary outside, with a light rain falling. *I won't overthink it—just go*, she thought.

"I'll call you tomorrow," she managed to say, because her friend had already pulled her away to dance.

Joanna looked at her watch; it was fifteen minutes after midnight. *I can make it to the subway*, she thought, quickening her pace. She walked down the street, lit by shop windows displaying clothes and, here and there, scantily clad mannequins. From time to time, she passed other late-night pedestrians.

I'm going to be completely soaked—I didn't even bring an umbrella, she thought, watching the large drops of water hit the pavement. The sound of footsteps splashing into puddles mixed with the gentle patter of the rain. With her head down, trying to step around the bigger puddles, she didn't notice the navy-blue van parked a few meters ahead of her. Two young men, maybe a few years older than her, got out. That's why she didn't cross the street, or at least move closer to the buildings for cover.

By the time she noticed them approaching her, it was too late. They immediately threw a bag over her head and dragged her into the van, which sped off with screeching tires. They threw her onto the floor of the vehicle.

She began to struggle and scream. Two strong arms held her legs. One man held her head, while the other pressed the bag against her mouth with his hand. She started to run out of breath, so she stopped screaming. The pressure eased, and she tried to cry out again—for help. Immediately, she felt him shove a rag so hard into her mouth that her entire palate ached. She tried to bite him, but her teeth only sank into the rough material of the bag. *Bastard*, she thought. She was so stunned that she couldn't even process what they might want from her.

Then she felt her legs being forced apart and hands tearing off her panties. The same hands moved upwards; she heard the rip of her torn blouse. The feeling of fingers grabbing her bra and the sharp tug as it was torn off made her realize what was coming. She arched her whole torso up, trying to throw off the disgusting body on top of her. She felt him inside her. She was still screaming, trying to shout, but instead of her own voice, she only heard his grunts. She lost her strength and gave up completely. She felt emptiness, a vast emptiness, and regret that this was happening to her.

"Why me?" she asked herself. She didn't feel pain, only his movements and a terrible rage at this degenerate who was doing this to her. Suddenly, he froze, his grip loosened, and she felt him pull away from her.

She didn't know how many of them there were, and with horror gripping her throat, she waited to see what would happen next.

The hands holding her head let go, but a moment later, they grabbed her sides and rolled her onto her stomach. Then, for a brief moment, there was a gap in the sack and she saw him. He was standing there with his pants down, legs spread. She can still see that face today.

"Not in the same hole," she heard.

"Me? It's a piece of cake," a nonchalant male voice said from behind her. She felt someone's hands grab her hips.

A sharp, piercing pain shot through her body.

"I'm suffocating," she screamed, but only a soft grunt escaped her throat.

"She's fine, yeah," her consciousness registered in the last second before she passed out. She sank into oblivion.

She was awakened by the rain. She was lying on wet ground. She was alone. She pulled the bag off her head and looked around. A courtyard and some garages. She struggled to her feet and pulled herself together enough to walk out to the street. She had no purse, no money, nothing. She doesn't remember how she got home. All she sees is her terrified mother and an outburst of tears at the sight of her.

CHAPTER I

JOANNA

Peter looked up from the briefcase he was searching. *Who is she? How did she get in here unannounced? I need to talk to Lola, our secretary,* he thought. The woman was dressed entirely in a beige suit, and her head was wrapped in a solid-colored scarf that matched it. Her eyes, hidden behind wide dark glasses, made her face and entire figure mysterious and unrecognizable.

He was having a bad day. He had just returned from the courthouse, where another controversial verdict had been passed. *How do they do it? Do they have no sense of reality?* he thought as he left the courtroom where his client, unable to believe his own ears, had heard the judgment.

"Come to my office tomorrow, we'll figure out what to do next," he'd said, then quickly left, torn between anger and hopelessness.

"Are you Mr. Piotr Głowacki?" a strong, confident voice asked.

"That's me. What can I do for you?"

"Is your office clean?" was the question.

"I think you can see for yourself," he replied, not very politely.

"No, you can't see it, but you can hear it. I'm talking about bugs."

He wasn't sure, so he answered honestly. "I don't know."

"Let's meet here," she said, handing him a piece of paper with a short sentence on it:

...Boulevard, bench by the sixth lamppost from the beach side, 10 a.m.

He wanted to say something else, but the stranger put a finger to her lips and left.

How does she know I'll come? he thought. But on the other hand, he was aware that he *would* go to this mysterious meeting. She had intrigued him by having the note ready.

"Aśka!" he called out.

The door opened and Aśka entered.

"Who was that?" Aśka asked first. "The secretary sent her to me, but she insisted on speaking with you."

"I have no idea."

"Is it clean here?"

"Mrs. Jadzia tries her best," she replied, amazed that he was interested in such mundane matters.

"Yes, I know. Let's go for coffee. I'm buying you a cappuccino and a fatty donut, just the way you like it," she said, taking him by the hand and leading him out into the office building corridor. Their office on the seventh floor on Main Street wasn't much different from the others in the building: two private offices, a conference room, a waiting area, several small rooms, and one large one with cubicles containing desks and computers for their permanent and temporary employees. Add a fairly large storage room, a secretariat at the entrance, and two utility rooms, and that was it. The entire wing of the office building had to be enough for them, and so far they had no complaints, except maybe about the fees they considered too high.

They took the elevator down to the snack bar in silence, ordered coffee and donuts, and sat at a round table in the corner.

"Is it clean here?" he repeated the question.

"What do you mean, Peter?" Aśka said.

"Are there bugs in our office? That woman was right," he added immediately. "She didn't want to talk to me when I said I didn't know. What kind of 'intelligence firm' are we without a clean room? We need to do something about it."

"I'll take care of it right away," she said. "Do you suspect we're being eavesdropped on, or even spied on?"

"I don't, but she does. She came in with that. Read this," he said, handing her the note. "She's cautious, so she must have something important, maybe even dangerous, to offer."

Aśka took the piece of paper and thought for a moment. Her analytical mind tried to extract some hidden information from it, but there was none in the short message.

"You have to go," she sighed. "I'll have your back. I'll take two people with me, maybe they can sniff something out."

He went to the meeting the next morning.

Sitting on the sixth bench on the Boulevard, Peter didn't expect the stranger who ran up to him with a light, sporty jog to be a graceful, athletic woman. Dressed in a tracksuit with the hood up, she stood next to him. He didn't recognize her at first, until she spoke and he heard that dominant voice.

"Keep me company," she said to him, taking off her large sunglasses for a moment. He saw her green eyes, and for a second, he was struck by the conviction that he had seen them somewhere before.

She started running again without waiting for his reaction.

He wasn't prepared for this kind of meeting. It was a sunny summer day, so he was dressed casually. Like most guys on the Boulevard, he wore jeans, a T-shirt, and sneakers. The unofficial nature of the meeting had dictated his attire.

I'm not going to wear a suit to the Boulevard; he had reasoned correctly that morning.

He got up from the bench and quickly ran after the stranger. When he caught up with her, she smiled at him.

"I'm Joanna K... from DLACOM," she introduced herself.

I'm such a fool for not connecting who came to see me right away, he thought, looking at the woman.

Peter couldn't have expected that someone from the top hundred richest people in the country would bother to approach him on their own. They always hired people for that. *It has to be something personal, and she wants to be discreet,* he thought as he jogged along behind her.

She hadn't chosen the location by chance. On one side was the sea, on the other, a large escarpment. No cars drove here, and there were no boats or motorboats visible nearby.

She's alone, without protection! he was surprised again, observing the area. She noticed him looking around.

"Are you surprised I'm alone?" she asked.

"Yes," he replied briefly, thus letting her know that he knew who she was.

They continued running at a light jog. Peter kept half a step behind, admiring her silhouette and the easy stride with which she ran, not looking back at him.

"I have a job for you," she finally got to the point. She reached into her tracksuit pocket and pulled out a business card. "This is my private number. Call me, and we'll arrange a meeting in my clean office." Without waiting for an answer, she quickened her pace, throwing over her shoulder, "See you."

He didn't chase her. He knew that was all for today.

"Aśka, where are you?" he asked into the microphone embedded in his shirt button. He sat down on a bench and waited. He didn't look at the business card she had given him; he would do that later in the office.

How did she find me? he wondered. He didn't advertise his services much. The company operated on word-of-mouth. They only had wealthy clients, which Aśka and her numerous contacts worked hard to secure.

He heard the sound of wheels on the concrete. It was Aśka, who rode up on her bike, braking lightly near his bench. Dressed like most Sunday cyclists who frequented the area, she blended into the background. She sat down next to him, took a water bottle from the bicycle frame, and started drinking.

"Talk," he heard between sips.

"She's the head of DLACOM. Call everyone off and let's go back to the office."

"Not so fast. It's getting interesting. She was being followed by some guy. He ran after her, and when she stopped next to you, he stopped too. I've already taken care of him–Tomasz is following him on a bike."

"Maybe it's her security," he suggested, although he knew Aśka was rarely wrong in such matters; her observations were usually flawless.

"No, her security is sitting in a car at the end of the Boulevard."

"How do you know?"

"I planted a bug on her, and I can hear what she's saying. We'll know more in a moment; she's just reaching the end of the Boulevard. She's getting into an Audi and heading downtown. She has her own office building there."

"Follow the tail, check who it is," she commanded, speaking into the microphone connected to the headphones she wore, which weren't just for listening to music.

"Let's go to the office," Peter said, standing up.

"No, it's impossible right now–they're tearing down the walls as we speak." She smiled at him with the smile that captivated everyone who had to deal with her. "Come to my place. They're cleaning the rooms at the office. It'll take all day. I also ordered one of the utility rooms to be converted into a 'quiet room' for the time being; that will take some time too."

"I'll meet you at the end of the Boulevard," she said over her shoulder and rode off.

As he walked, he thought about how it could be that *she* had come to him. Not to their office, not to Aśka, but directly to him. He didn't know her, nor had he ever dealt with her IT giant or any of its subsidiaries.

Yet her face seemed familiar. He had seen her picture in various magazines or on TV, so now he couldn't remember anything specific. But this thought haunted him all the way to the end of the Boulevard.

Aśka returned the rental bike, and they walked to her apartment. She had a nice, cozy place nearby. For a woman in her thirties, she looked great, though her beauty wasn't the type the media typically portrayed. He liked it, and Aśka appreciated that, though they had never ended up in bed together.

"For now," she always told him when he tried to get closer at the beginning of their partnership. He had to back off then because it was becoming awkward, and he valued her and their collaboration too much.

They spent the rest of the day going through every possible piece of information about *her*. They didn't find anything interesting beyond publicly available data from the stock market, magazines, tabloids, and IT industry publications.

Peter walked confidently into the spacious lobby of the DLACOM office building, located on one of the main streets in the city center. He now knew much more about the company and its owner and main shareholder.

She has her office here, he thought. She's from this city, and she has a residence not far from the forest.

"Piotr Głowacki," he introduced himself. "I have an appointment with the President." He glanced at the receptionist but saw no particular interest in her expression. His name meant nothing here.

"Please follow me; the Boss is waiting for you."

He looked at his watch. *Am I late?* No, he was five minutes early. Punctuality was a good trait in their profession, highly desirable. He followed the girl, noting her long legs in high heels. The sound of her heels echoed through the hall as they walked toward the elevator.

They took the elevator to the very top. Getting out, he noticed an inscription on the wall: *12th Floor.*

Interesting. There were only 11 buttons in the elevator–he was sure because he had counted them on the way up. Access to the 12th floor must be controlled from the reception desk or her secretariat.

She occupied the entire 12th floor. They passed several doors until the receptionist led him to a wide branch of the corridor ending in frosted glass sliding doors. The girl placed her right hand into a recess in the wall, and a moment later the doors slid silently open, revealing a corridor leading to her office. He looked curiously at the stylishly decorated hallway, tasteful but without ostentation. Three paintings hung on the wall; one depicted a familiar rural landscape with horses in the background. *Probably a Kossak,* he had no doubt it was an original.

Then he saw her. She rose from behind a large desk and walked toward him with her hand outstretched. The receptionist disappeared without a trace.

"Hello, Peter," she said. "I think I can still call you that."

"Still"–a warning light went on in his head.

"Of course," he confirmed. "And when did the President start talking to me like that?" he asked, not very assertively.

"You danced with me all evening at the Carnival Ball at our school."

At these words, his memory unlocked instantly.

"Joasia, for God's sake, is that YOU? How many years has it been? I would never have guessed it was you if you hadn't mentioned our Ball. I didn't recognize you–I'm sorry."

"Sit down, please." She took his hand and led him to a round table with three comfortable armchairs and a neat sofa.

She sat opposite him and smiled, seeing the impression her words had made.

"I'm sorry I didn't recognize you right away in my office."

"You couldn't have. I was dressed so you wouldn't recognize me. Something was nagging at me the whole time; I just didn't connect your image with... myself."

"Congratulations on the bug," she said.

"You know about it?" he was surprised.

"Not right away. The sensors only picked it up when I came inside."

"I'm sorry. If I had known... I don't need that now. They attached it to you before you gave me your card. By the time I found out, you were already in your car."

"Who did it?"

"A girl on a bicycle," he explained.

"I didn't notice anything, but it wouldn't have mattered anyway. I never mix my private life with my professional life, especially when it comes to clothes."

"Let's have a drink to our meeting," she said, getting up from her chair. She walked across the room to a burgundy door that looked like a bookcase, behind which a bar was hidden. "What will you have?"

"In the morning? Coffee with a little cognac, please."

She poured him coffee and cognac, and herself a glass of wine.

This emphasizes the private nature of our meeting, he thought. He didn't ask anything, knowing she would get to the point herself.

She sat comfortably, crossing her legs, looked into his eyes, and began to speak.

"I saw you on a TV show a couple of months ago. That's how I know what you do. I also know you can keep a secret. You never revealed ours, even though I was so afraid you would at the time. I was terrified the whole school would find out we slept together after that Ball."

Why is she telling me this? he thought. For him, it had been an episode of little importance. She had dragged him to bed herself, and he hadn't resisted. That was all he remembered from what she was describing.

"That's one of the most beautiful memories of my life, because it happened before... what happened to me two weeks later," she continued, a hint of pain in her voice. "I was a snot-nosed teenager, and you were a school graduate, three years older than me. A whole era separated us back then, but you took an interest in me and stayed with me until the end of the Ball, and a little longer."

She smiled at him again. She leaned over and put her hand on his. "Please, help me," she said simply.

He didn't remember much more about what she was talking about. He knew he had slept with some seventeen-year-old girl, partly because he'd had a fight with his girlfriend and broken up with her. Apparently, Joasia remembered those moments differently.

"I'll do everything in my power," he assured her, covering her hand with his other hand. She didn't pull away.

"You don't even know how much you meant to me then," she said, more to herself than to him.

As if through a fog, he vaguely recalled walking around the school looking for her, asking her friends about her.

"I was looking for you then, but you'd disappeared," he said, not entirely sure it was true.

"I know you were looking. You were a good guy."

"At first I thought you were the father. I even wanted it so badly, but it wasn't you–unfortunately," she added in a worried voice.

He stiffened, froze, completely walled off. *What is this?* he thought.

She noticed his nervousness. She stroked his hand and, looking warmly into his eyes, said in a calm tone, "Everything that happened to me later doesn't concern you. I know that. I'm absolutely sure of it."

"Wait a minute!" She got up and walked over to the desk. As he watched her go, he thought he would like to go back to the night he'd slept with her. He didn't remember much from that night. It would be worth recalling.

She placed an envelope on the table. "See what's inside."

He took a DHL envelope and pulled out green coral beads–a small string of them. About twenty pieces strung together. He didn't count them. They meant nothing to him.

"There are 28 in the envelope. I was wearing them at our Ball, but there were more then. I was also wearing them two weeks later, when I was raped... 28 years ago."

He shifted restlessly. This was not the news he had expected. He was silent, not knowing how to react. Everything he wanted to say seemed petty and out of place, so he said nothing. After a moment, he managed, "I'm so very sorry."

She reached for her wine and drank the rest in one gulp. Then she continued.

"That's why I disappeared from school. My parents took me to my grandmother's. I was in a very bad state. They didn't report it to the police, and I had to face it alone. But no, that was the worst. The worst was yet to come."

She stood up and began pacing nervously around the room, clasping and unclasping her hands.

"When I realized I was pregnant, I was already in my fifth month. I was living like a zombie, walking around in a daze. I know now I was in shock and terribly depressed. I had no one to turn to. Then I started looking for you, thinking you were the father. But you had left town to study; that's all I managed to find out then. I couldn't accept that I was pregnant by a rapist. So throughout the pregnancy, I told myself it was yours. I was seriously ill. My parents didn't know anything about you, so they assumed the pregnancy was a result of the rape. I stayed at home for the last three months. I didn't go anywhere. I didn't even see a doctor–I wanted to die. On the day I went into labor, my father drove me to the hospital."

"An older, wise doctor there took an interest in my condition, and I confided everything in him. He treated my depression and advised my parents to consider adoption. I relinquished my parental rights. When I gave birth to a girl a few hours later–that's all I knew–they didn't show her to me. That evening, I ran away from the hospital and never went back. After a month, I was stable enough to continue my studies."

"I pushed that period out of my memory. Until now."

She got up again, walked to the bar, and poured herself more wine.

He approached her. "That must have been incredibly hard for you," he said, pouring himself a shot of vodka, which he downed immediately.

"That's not all–it got even worse."

"Two months after I left the hospital, my parents died in a train accident. They were on their way to visit me at university."

"I fell into a kind of lethargy again, and only my studies kept me going. I lived with my mother's parents. When they both passed away within a short time, I was completely alone. Recently, in their country house, I found my mother's diary in the attic. I never knew my mother kept a diary." She walked to the desk and pulled out a small, worn brown suitcase. It looked out of place, with rubbed corners and edges worn by age.

She carefully placed it on the table and opened the two brass clasps. Lifting the lid, she revealed the interior, lined with a faded silk-like material, with three large notebooks lying at the bottom.

"This one is for you," she said, handing him one of them. "Those," she nodded at the other two, "have nothing to do with this case. They're from earlier."

"Open it," she asked, as if she didn't have the strength to do it herself.

He turned over the hard cover of the notebook. The first page had a date and neat, careful handwriting filling the entire page. He flipped through a few more pages. Nothing but dates and entries written in the same hand.

"Look at the end."

He opened to the last page. A plain gray envelope was glued there, with an inscription:

FOR JOASIA

Peter looked inside. He pulled out two locks of blonde hair, each tied with a different colored ribbon. Inside was also a half-sheet of notepaper with the following written in the same handwriting:

Angel One.

Angel Two.

JOASIA'S CHILDREN.

On the other side were the names of several cities with streets, and at the bottom, girls' names and numbers. The rest of the page was filled with similar, seemingly meaningless information. Next to most names were two or three numbers, with others only one

Poznań, 17 Twarda St.

Zofia – 7, 14

Julia – 6, 8, 11

He read the last entry. Then he put the paper back in the envelope and looked at Joanna questioningly.

She stood up and walked slowly to the center of the room. A moment passed before she spoke again.

"When I found this, all the memories came flooding back. I realized I must have given birth to twin girls, and my mother had kept locks of their hair for me. I don't know what these numbers, city names, and streets mean, even though I've spent a lot of time on it. I can't connect the numbers to anything on this paper or anywhere else."

"I was already independent and financially secure, so I hired a detective agency to find my daughters."

"I wasted a whole year. The only thing they were able to determine was that you are not related to the owner of that hair." She smiled at him again. "A pity, because I had hoped you were all along."

He got up and walked to the bar. "May I?" he asked.

"Of course."

He poured himself a vodka and drank the whole glass in one gulp. After a moment, he did it again.

He sat down.

She continued to look at him warmly and seemed somewhat amused.

"I would like you to find the sender of these packages–I think it's the bastard who raped me. How and what he knows about me; I have no idea. Maybe he recognized me in a newspaper photo, or maybe he's been nearby all this time."

"Is he blackmailing you?" he asked.

"No, there was nothing inside except the coral beads."

"I'm so sorry, Joasia," he said at last.

"Don't be. You don't owe me anything."

"I believe you'll help me find my daughters and catch that bastard. I'm not a defenseless teenager anymore," she said in a hard, strong voice. "I can be dangerous to anyone," she added, though she didn't explain what she meant.

I don't doubt that, he thought. She wouldn't have achieved what she had if she were soft.

"Now let's move on to more mundane matters," he heard.

"Namely?"

"Your fee. I want you to devote all your time to this–I have a feeling something bad is happening. Are you working on anything else?"

"Yes, but others will handle those matters. I will personally handle this case with my closest collaborator, Aśka. In a way, this concerns me too," he added.

"I'm glad you see it that way."

"To start, you'll receive 100,000 złoty, and I will cover all expenses related to this job. Don't interrupt," she said, seeing him about to speak. "If you find my daughters, the bonus will be 200,000 for each. And if you find this bastard, you'll get another 200,000."

"You're too generous," he managed to interject.

"I can afford it. And you're worth it. I'm never wrong about people. The contract will be delivered to your office; all you have to do is sign it."

"How much time do I have?" he asked.

"I don't know. I received this the day before yesterday. That's why I came to you right away."

She handed him another DHL envelope. Inside were three loose green beads from her necklace and three photos. Two showed her at a party. The third showed her getting out of a car, with some people standing nearby.

"Are you being followed?"

"Yes. That's why we're talking here."

"Did you report it to the police?"

"Don't joke!"

"I only ask pro forma. Who else knows about all this?"

"No one."

"And the private detective?"

"He'll be quiet, but he only knows a part. His job was to find the children and check your DNA. He doesn't know who I am or who gave the order. I never spoke to him or contacted him directly. He received the order from one of our law firms in England."

"Good, that's very good. It makes the task easier," he said. But he was wrong, very wrong.

"I'm suspending all my professional affairs. I am at your disposal full-time while you handle this matter. Call me and come whenever you want, day or night. Do you know where I live?"

He nodded.

She walked over to Peter, embraced him, and hugged him as if those twenty-something years had never passed.

"Go now. I need to cry," she whispered in his ear.

She must be very lonely, he thought as he left. The same girl was waiting for him by the hallway door.

Joanna K. hadn't lost her self-confidence in many years. But now, talking to Piotr, she felt something she had only experienced when she'd been with him years ago. Sobbing quietly, she tried to calm herself. His face, his voice, the way he looked at her–it all reminded her of the crazy days she'd spent with him. She had been in love for the first time, with the unvarnished love of a seventeen-year-old girl for an older boy from her school.

They didn't move in the same circles of friends. But he was friends with her older cousin, Aga, who sometimes took Joanna to student parties that Peter also attended. It was then that she fell madly in love with him.

"Why do you need him?" Aga had tried to dissuade her. "Guys his age aren't interested in younger girls, but older ones. You have no chance of a lasting relationship." When she learned from Aga that he had broken up with his girlfriend, she decided to "attack" Peter. He would never have noticed her on his own.

She could still feel the emotions that had overwhelmed her when she dared to approach him for the first time in the university library. She didn't remember the title of the book, but she remembered his gaze perfectly as he looked her up and down. The appraisal was apparently successful, because in a soft, velvety voice he asked, "Did you want a summary, or to borrow it?"

"No, I wanted to ask you out. That's why I came here to see you," she had said, looking him straight in the eye.

"Aren't you a little young for that?" he replied, smiling, tickled by her boldness.

"What can a young woman give you that an old one won't–you know the saying," she went all in.

"You're feisty."

"Maybe a little. But I like clear situations. It's Peter, right?" she asked. "Will you give me a chance?"

"For what?"

"To get to know me better. I'm Joanna," she said, holding out her hand to him.

He took her hand, squeezing it lightly. He had very delicate hands with long, shapely fingers and, as she managed to notice, well-groomed nails that many women would envy.

He nodded unconsciously before speaking. "Let's go somewhere else; you can't talk here."

They went to a small pub on the same street. It was already afternoon; they sat at a small table for two, drank wine, and talked. To their mutual surprise, they found many common topics and interests, one of which was a love of dance. That's how the idea to go together to the school's Carnival Ball was born.

"And what does your girlfriend say?" she asked directly, pretending not to know about their breakup.

"Nothing–we're not together anymore."

Peter's ex-girlfriend was her opposite–a tall, shapely blonde with prominent breasts and full lips, popular with half the university. This made her self confident, and she dressed to show it off. At every event, a new admirer would latch onto her. Among them, she had a very unpleasant nickname–"Zlut."

At a previous event, Joanna had used that nickname. It was when "Zlut" had insulted her after they bumped into each other on the dance floor. She called Joanna a "mouthy brat" and called security to have her thrown out of the student party at the "Quiet Cellar," whose name was the opposite of what went on there.

Joanna never gave up on a goal once she set it, except for that one time in the hospital–but then she had been ill and terribly depressed.

Today she felt the same as she had back then in the library.

What is happening? she asked herself. The memories came back, and the feelings for him hadn't gone away all these years–that was her answer.

Peter returned to the office, surprised by the meeting. He patiently answered Aśka's many questions, telling her about the meeting with Joanna and the commission he had undertaken.

"I don't understand something," Aśka said, pacing the room with a glass of tea in her hand.

"What don't you understand?"

"Why did she only now start looking for her daughters? She's had the financial means to hire the best people in our industry for a long time. I'm sure they would have found something by now."

"She only just found her mother's diary."

"But the child was born earlier. Damn, I don't know, I don't understand how anyone could give up their own child."

"Half their own," he interjected between sips of tea.

"The other half of the genes belong to the child's father. We have to assume those are the rapist's genes."

"What are you talking about, Peter?" she waved her hand at him, expressing her disagreement with the gesture. "Are you sure about that?" she asked, standing in front of him and looking him in the eye.

"I'm not sure of anything. I don't remember much from those days."

"Maybe it was different," she said, trying to question the sequence of events he had accepted.

"I don't think so."

"And yet—there could be several versions. Maybe at the party, someone drugged her, or got her drunk, and she went to bed with someone without knowing who..." she began to fantasize, until he interrupted her.

"Stop it, that doesn't make sense. We'll check her version carefully, and then we'll know how it really was."

Calmed down, she stopped pacing the room. She sat in an armchair, placed her laptop on her knees, and started searching the internet.

"Let's start with the easiest part."

"Namely?"

"The train disaster."

When it came to computers, the internet, and everything related, he didn't interfere, knowing Aśka would extract all the information they needed. There was no better specialist in their company than her.

He sighed and got up from his chair. "Work well. I'll take care of the tails."

She didn't even notice when he left.

When Peter called Joanna, he didn't think it would be a turning point in his life. He was alone; he had long since realized his lifestyle wasn't conducive to lasting relationships, and the women in his life didn't share his passion for his work. It always ended the same way. The breakups were painful, so he stopped getting involved in serious relationships, limiting his needs to brief encounters that naturally fizzled out when he kept saying, "I don't have time," or "We'll see each other later."

"Peter, I'm glad you called. I was upset about how we parted. I was about to call you."

"That would have been nice, but I beat you to it."

Joanna sat on the edge of her jacuzzi, rubbing cream into her legs. She had been waiting for this call impatiently. She would have called him sooner but was afraid of scaring him away. She knew nothing about his private life. Back when she had his DNA checked, she hadn't wanted to know anything, afraid she would be disappointed. However, when he appeared in her office, she was surprised to find she was still infatuated with him. The memories came flooding back–*Do I still love him?* she had asked herself an hour ago while lying in the warm water.

"I have something. Can I come over? It's not for the phone."

She jumped up instantly. *Oh my God, I won't have time to get dressed,* she thought, saying, "Of course, I'll be waiting."

She called security.

When he drove up to the huge gate, flanked by two red brick towers with pointed turrets, he noticed a camera lens tracking him. He didn't stop or get out, but drove forward as the gate opened, revealing a wide, paved road. On the security building just inside, on the left, a red sign lit up: STOP. Out of the corner of his eye, he saw the claws of a barrier retracting from across the road. When they disappeared completely, the sign changed to green: CLEAR.

He moved on. He saw two bodyguards emerge from the guardhouse–they approached him. He rolled down the window and said, "Piotr Głowacki. I have an appointment."

"Please proceed," he heard, so he moved forward. But he managed to see a flash–*they're taking pictures,* he thought.

He drove along the road through a beautifully maintained garden leading up to Joanna's mansion itself. A large, single-story building, constructed in a modern, slightly avant-garde style, was integrated into the garden surrounding the entire residence.

Joanna was already standing at the door. *She was waiting for me,* he thought as he walked up the path.

He walked toward her with a quick, confident step, admiring her shapely figure with pleasure. *She looks quite different here than in her office–more approachable,* he noted.

"Hello, Peter," she said, shaking his hand in greeting. When he surprised her by pulling a huge bouquet of red roses from behind his back, she embraced him and kissed him on the cheek.

"Thank you, they're beautiful."

"But not as beautiful as you," he blurted out.

She looked at him, and it was obvious the compliment pleased her.

"That's how I like you... I *liked* you," she corrected herself quickly.

But Peter didn't miss the first wording.

She took him by the hand, saying, "Come on, breakfast is waiting."

"Thank you, I've already eaten."

"But I haven't."

She led him into the living room and from there into a spacious dining room, with a kitchenette visible at the back.

"The house has two wings," she explained. "One for guests, and the other for me. In this one, I do everything myself. I like it," she added, somewhat unnecessarily.

Peter didn't know much about interior design, but what he saw completely surprised him. *Where did this come from?* he thought, looking at the dining room with its annex. Everything seemed normal, yet the unusual combinations of styles and colors harmonized with the décor of the walls and furniture.

"It's my soul," she said, seeing him look around.

"Beautiful, great taste," he emphasized his admiration, gesturing around them.

"Make yourself comfortable. I'll serve everything right away."

She had everything ready. Two bowls of vegetable salads, a platter of cold cuts and seafood were already on the table, and moments later, delicious, fragrant buns and croissants landed.

"Would you like something warm?" she asked.

"No, thank you," he said, narrowing his eyes slightly and frowning at the same time. He looked at her as a woman he was attracted to but didn't want to reveal himself in front of her.

However, she noticed his gaze. He had looked at her that way before. Instinctively, she adjusted a lock of hair that had fallen on her forehead.

She was wearing a long skirt with a deep slit on the side that revealed her long legs with every step. A blouse made of a slightly shimmering material and discreet jewelry emphasized her beauty. She intimidated him, so he secretly examined her figure.

She looked at him and smiled. "You haven't changed over the years. You know, you scanned me from head to toe like that before," she joked.

"No, I don't remember that," he admitted honestly.

"It was at the beginning, in the university library, where we met."

"I find that hard to forget."

Involuntarily, he glanced at her hand as she poured him tea.

She noticed because she said, "I don't have one!"

"Don't have what?"

"A wedding ring."

"You're smart, you always have been," he added.

"I don't have one either," he said with a smile.

They both laughed, which immediately eased the tension.

"Well, we've clarified that issue."

"Yesterday I found out that..."

She put two fingers to his lips. "Later," she asked. "I don't often have the chance to have breakfast here with a man. And with you, it will only be the fourth time."

He didn't remember the three previous times, but he didn't comment. They were alone; music from the hits of their youth oozed from somewhere in the distance.

Joanna ate slowly, as if she wanted these moments to last longer than the time they should reasonably devote to a meal. Peter spread butter and a little blackcurrant jam on a bun. He ate more for company than out of hunger. He glanced furtively at Joanna, not wanting to spoil the moment. A snobbish thought crossed his mind–*how many guys can boast of having eaten breakfast with her in her own home?*

"Peter, you're not angry with me, are you?" Joanna's voice snapped him out of his thoughts, referring to his visit to her office.

"Of course not."

"Those memories were too much for me–I cried, and it was a relief."

"I understand."

"Then let's go," she said, seeing he had finished eating and was waiting for her to finish breakfast.

She was the first to get up from the table and waited for him to rise. With a smile on her lips, looking into his eyes, she walked up to him.

"Do you like gardens?" she asked, taking his arm.

"I don't have one myself, but I'd love to see yours."

"I'm not a snob or a mannered celebrity. I haven't changed that much over the years. Only the environment around me has changed."

"I'll show you the house later," she said, and they stepped outside through a wide glass sliding door directly onto the terrace, where three tables stood. Flower beds, trees, and short-cut grass were everywhere, as well as a large pool with blue water that invited a morning swim.

"Sit down. I'm very curious about what you've found."

At that moment, a figure of a girl in a white apron appeared from around the corner with a tray in her hands. She placed coffee, a large glass of cognac, and a glass of white wine on the table. She nodded and disappeared.

"This is our morning coffee. That's all I know about what you like in the morning," she said in a tone that suggested it was his fault she knew so little about him.

"Talk," she asked, settling comfortably into a wicker chair. She tucked her legs underneath herself, then after a moment shifted them to the side of the table so Peter could easily look at them.

"How often do you run on the Boulevard?" he asked.

"Three or four times a week when I'm in town."

"Can you do the same route tomorrow?"

"Yes, of course, but why?" She didn't like repeating questions, but now she had to restrain her impatience so as not to offend him.

"When I met you on the Boulevard, we picked up your tail."

"I already know that"–she didn't like having to repeat things twice. She had an excellent memory, which sometimes surprised people when she repeated their words from years ago, so she was irritated by every repeated sentence.

"Following you, my operative noticed he wasn't the only one. However, we weren't prepared for that, so he lost them on the City Ring Road. You can't follow someone there on a bike," he explained the reason for losing the tail. "But we got the car's license plate. He might have taken pictures of you, too. Our guy, passing him on his bike, noticed a camera with a telephoto lens on the passenger seat." After a moment, he added with slight pride, "The car's owner is a former traffic policeman. He was fired five years ago for taking bribes but avoided trial. Apparently, he shared the proceeds with someone higher up. He doesn't live at his registered address; we don't know who he works for yet, but we'll find out. Now we'll be prepared for anything. So we know you're being followed, and it might be the same man who took those photos of you. But he's certainly not involved in what happened years ago; he's too young. I have one more question?"

"Yes, I'm listening."

"I started reading your mother's diary. There are many personal, very personal entries, reflections, and observations. I'm not sure if I should continue reading it?"

"You must," she interrupted him. "I've read it, many times, but I didn't discover anything. My perspective is too personal. However, I had the impression that there was something there, some important information I was missing because I couldn't be objective."

"Okay, you're the boss here," he joked. A second later, he realized he might have offended her.

"I'm sorry, I didn't mean anything by it."

"I know. But I don't always want to 'be the boss.' I'd like to be seen as an ordinary woman. Must every guy look at me through the media's prism?"

"I don't see you that way. More like..." He paused mid-sentence, considering whether to admit the thoughts haunting him.

"Finish your thought."

"Not like that."

"Please, tell me."

"When I looked at you today, I felt sorry for those moments before the breakfasts you mentioned, because I don't remember all of them." He was becoming more talkative. "You're a beautiful, attractive woman, and I'm not at all surprised I paid attention to you back then. You wanted it yourself," he added, cutting his confession short.

But Joanna liked how he said it. She felt he was sincere, just a little intimidated. She also knew men often felt overwhelmed by her strong personality. She didn't want Peter to react that way, so she confessed honestly, "I miss those breakfasts, too."

He looked at her with a gaze that said, *what are we waiting for?* but completely different words came out of his mouth. "Do you have paparazzi under your window?"

"There are always some people hanging around here. Be prepared, I am," she said. She wasn't expecting such words, so she got up from her chair and stood behind him. Placing both hands on his shoulders, she whispered, "It doesn't matter. The important thing is that you're here now."

He knew if he stood up now, they would start kissing, so he remained seated. He wasn't ready yet. He didn't know what to make of all this; besides, she intimidated him.

"You intimidate me," he said, turning his head toward her.

"Me?"

"No, not you, but your position."

"Peter, I'm the same girl I was when I fell in love with you, except now I have a lot of money."

"Exactly!"

She twisted a lock of his hair with her hand–*she used to do that,* he remembered.

"Peter, can't you see anything?"

"I see, and it scares me."

"Unnecessarily."

"And yet."

She sensed his anxiety and let go. She knew what he was saying was true, and she knew that sooner or later he would fall into her arms; it was only a matter of time. She always achieved what she wanted. Now she would wait until *he* wanted the same thing she did. She could see him looking at her, so she calmed her desire to go to bed with him right then and there. *Waiting for what is about to happen is also exciting.*

CHAPTER II
PARTY

Piotr received an invitation—not from his former bosses at the law firm where he had worked a few years back, but from Karol, a lawyer friend from his university days.

It was his third, and what would likely be his last, party billed as an "integration meeting," though "secret gathering" would have been a more fitting name.

Several dozen people showed up at the remote forester's lodge in the Tri-City Sightseeing Park. The guests practiced professions as lawyers, legal advisors, judges, prosecutors, and two bailiffs—one of whom was related to a judge and worked at the very same court as his brother. Just your typical informal, family-style arrangements funded by the state.

What for? Why are these events held like closed impeachment hearings? he had wondered at the first one. But after that initial meeting, his surprise had worn off, replaced by understanding.

His introduction to this inner circle hadn't come from his boss at the firm, but from Brygida, his lover at the time—a slightly older legal advisor employed by an international company. She did it for herself, not for him. She wanted to show off her new "toy." Those were the very words that had slipped from her after a few drinks.

Being completely unprepared for this "Masonic" congress of Themis's representatives and the legal profession, he was taken aback by the presence of judges, prosecutors, advocates, and several top legal advisors from major Tri-City firms. The thing that struck him was the complete absence of anyone outside the profession. No wives, husbands, lovers, or mistresses who weren't active practitioners themselves.

Many of the lawyers, judges, and prosecutors he knew weren't there. He probably never would have received this "grace" if not for Brygida.

An unwritten law governed the place; perhaps they even had a code of conduct dictating who could do what and what their place was in this informal union of "Sacred Cows"—as he came to call them, though he didn't know it at the time.

After a few hours, when the party was in full swing and spirits were high, a slightly disheveled District Court judge from the Family Division, dancing with him and reminiscing about the "good old days" of communism, whispered in his ear that she had been invited by her boss. This likely meant the President of the Court had invited her to a well-known resort near Warsaw for a nationwide meeting of this not-quite-reputable group.

It was after that party that he decided to break from this profession. He had no desire to become one of *them*.

Karol, his friend from college who came from a multi-generational family of lawyers, after consuming a sea of alcohol, made Piotr understand why he had lost a seemingly straightforward case. Maybe not so straightforward, after all: on one side of the courtroom had sat a attorney for Senator G..., and on the other, Piotr, representing a young businessman.

"There couldn't have been any other verdict," Karol slurred. "That attorney has been coming here for ten years. My father was still coming with him back in the day." Then he reached for his glass, drank, and went on. "And the judge who presided over your case? She's only been attending these meetings for three years, and she's very eager to get a promotion to the District Court."

Hearing this, Piotr stopped wondering why the verdicts in cases involving judges he knew from these events always seemed to favor the other side.

The same applied to the Prosecutor's Office and other representatives of this supposedly blind Lady Justice.

These people in court robes were here to determine the *who*, *when*, and *with whom*—so that later, it was easy to agree on the *HOW MUCH*!

The corrupt environment of these Sacred Cows, operating like an Indian bazaar, felt completely untouchable. It was here that you could essentially "order" a verdict in a specific case, a discontinuation of proceedings, or a dismissal with a finding that the action "bore no hallmarks of a crime."

"Do you think, Piotr, that it even needs to be justified properly?" he asked himself.

Yes, it should be—he answered his own thought. But all they have to do is call white black, and what can anyone do to a judge like that? Nothing. Absolutely nothing.

"You can appeal to a higher court," Piotr argued.

"Oh, you can *claim* that," Karol retorted. "Yes, you can file an appeal. But what you don't know is that the files for these 'Sacred Cows' are specially flagged. No judge, no panel of judges, would dare to overturn a verdict and oppose this informal group."

"Of course, this privilege isn't for everyone. It's an option reserved for the connected—whether they're gangsters, businessmen, or so-called liberal professionals. And if anyone threatens to expose them, they all cry in unison about an 'attack on their independence,' which is just a code for their financial independence."

"The privileged caste of Sacred Cows is doing just fine. And if any of them gets tired of the scams, they can always retire with a full state pension and then go earn a second salary on the side at some private law firm."

"There is one exception—the military bar. They operate outside these arrangements. Not because they're part of some 'barrack-room Themis'—the very idea of their independence is a joke—but because they have their own separate deals and hierarchies." Karol roared this into Piotr's ear, competing with the loud music and his own drunkenness.

"It's our eternal rivalry, you see. The two systems don't mix. That doesn't mean there are no Sacred Cows over there. They exist, but they wear uniforms and have different priorities. It's like that recent incident at the press conference, where one of their representatives took a shot at another and hit a shield instead. How he ended up in that situation is another story, but not as unrelated as you might think," he chuckled again, lost in a drunken haze.

A moment later, Karol stopped his lecture because his head slumped onto the table. He fell asleep quickly and unexpectedly, his restless, uncontrolled snoring confirming his state. No one was bothered by the noise; everyone was too preoccupied with their own affairs.

Piotr got up and left the party without even saying goodbye to Brygida. He ignored her calls afterward until she finally gave up. In a way, he was grateful to her. She was the one who had ultimately pushed him to establish his own company and step away from the traditional attorney's path.

It was then that he began looking more deeply into the lost case Karol had mentioned. With the help of colleagues and access to certain files, he discovered a disturbing pattern in all matters connected to Senator G.

What he found was terrifying: routine alterations of witness testimony, the admission of inadmissible evidence, documents disappearing from case files, forgeries fabricated by the Senator's lawyers, perjured witness statements, falsified signatures, fabricated wiretap recordings, and witness intimidation.

The sheer audacity of the Senator's legal team was epitomized by an incident involving a university colleague of Piotr's. When this colleague learned about Piotr's investigation, he confronted him at a coffee bar downstairs.

"Mind if I join?" he asked, not waiting for an answer before pulling up a chair.

"You're digging for something you'll never find," he began grimly.

"About what?"

"About the Senator G. files."

"How do you know?"

"Everyone knows what you're doing outside the bar."

"So?"

"Let me tell you what happened recently. Some of the Senator's... associates approached me. As I was walking from the court to the parking lot, a guy came up to me and got straight to the point. He said, 'You're defending Mr. Nowak in the payment case against Gigant Company. Our principal will pay you five times your fee to lose this lawsuit. "

"What did you do?" Piotr asked.

"I told him to go to hell, though I regret I couldn't get it on record."

"And then?"

"I lost the case anyway. He just found other... supporters. But I got my fee, so I didn't care in the end," he said cynically.

Returning home, Piotr sat down at his computer, pondering the scale of this corruption. He typed a search into Google: "Scandals in the Tri-City justice system."

What he read only confirmed what he already knew. *These are just the ones that got caught,* he thought. If statistics were to be believed, the undetected cases likely constituted the vast majority. The most disturbing fact was that almost every scandal had only seen the light of day thanks to investigative journalists.

The state apparatus's response to these exposures was always swift and devastating: they would try to destroy the journalist at all costs, unleashing a barrage of civil and criminal lawsuits. They would also use wiretaps and surveillance to expose their sources.

And when a scandal could no longer be covered up, and only under immense public pressure, would there be any consequences. In just one of the Gdańsk Themis scandals, judges, prosecutors, and gangsters were indicted. Twenty-seven people were charged with ninety counts, including corruption, bribery, perversion of justice, abuse of power, and more.

And what was the result?

And nothing! Fellow judges refused to preside over the trial, and the Supreme Court seemed more concerned with the rights of the defendants than with justice for the victims.

He kept reading, moving on to scandals in the District Courts of Gdynia and Sopot. It seemed there wasn't a single court in the Tri-City that was clean—meaning the "black sheep" were working in every one of them.

He then broadened his search to the entire Pomeranian region, as if he hadn't learned enough already. Here, the scale of the problem was even greater.

"The Słupsk affair, the Pruszcz Gdański case... It's enough. I'm not going to keep cataloging the symptoms of this corruption within Themis and the legal profession across the whole country," he thought, and angrily turned off the computer.

"The problem has deeper roots," he continued to consider. "The system itself is flawed, allowing for a complete lack of oversight over these 'Sacred Cows.' This isn't about attacking their independence; it's about demanding they be held accountable, just like any other citizen. The awareness that they have immunity and operate without real control leads to scandals on this scale—and these are just the ones we know about. For anyone paying attention, it's no secret there are many more."

"Nepotism in the courts—this is almost never discussed, but it's another major cause of corrupt rulings. It also puts pressure on fundamentally honest judges, preventing them from issuing fair verdicts."

"Just imagine," he fumed, his humor turning sour, "how can you properly convict a bailiff, a notorious scoundrel, for fraud when his own brother is a judge in the very court handling the case? The judge assigned to the proceedings knows both brothers well; they've socialized for years. He *could* recuse himself, but that would be seen as an act of disloyalty to his fellow judge. So he doesn't. And of course, he rules in the bailiff's favor. That's a real example from the court in Słupsk."

"And what recourse does their victim have?" he muttered sullenly. "None. They're completely powerless."

Walking away from the computer, he made himself a promise: he would expose every such irregularity he came across, whatever the cost. However, he would not accept every job that involved taking on the Sacred Cows. He had to choose his battles.

CHAPTER III
INTELLIGENCE

Aśka had long since grown accustomed to her business partner's numerous romances. She didn't judge him, but rather the "beauties" he surrounded himself with. She knew he was wounded, badly scarred by the Woman of His Life— she had left him for money. Back then, he was a freshly minted lawyer with little to his name, and she hadn't wanted to wait any longer for him to strike it rich.

That was when Aśka had met him, and they had been a team ever since. Of course, only as business partners and associates, as he had made her a partner in the company. Although she held a smaller share, she still considered herself lucky to have found him and not some venal lawyer.

When she first saw Piotr, she had just turned eighteen a few days before. Thrilled to finally be entering adult life, she was making big plans for the future. She wanted to go to university, but her parents couldn't afford it, so she took on any odd job she could find.

It was during one such freelance job that she got into trouble.

Trying to earn some extra cash, she was working for a company that had tasked her with salvaging anything of value from a batch of old computers. Where the boss had gotten them, she had no idea. She quickly realized, however, that the hard drives had been intentionally and thoroughly destroyed and were practically unusable. Yet, on a few of them, data had been preserved through workarounds. In several units, floppy disks were still stuck in the drives.

What a mess, she thought. If they wanted to destroy the data, they should have shredded and melted the drives. That's the only sure way to erase everything.

Curious, she removed the hard drive that seemed most likely to contain data and connected it to a test computer, into which she inserted one of the floppy disks. It didn't work. Annoyed that something dared to challenge her abilities as a programmer and hobbyist hacker, she connected it to her private server and, using a program she had written herself, managed to partially access its contents.

She found herself looking at classified reports from the WSI (Military Intelligence Services), filled with names, numbers, code names, and other information she didn't fully understand. The floppy disk contained personal data on WSI employees, including their suitability for service and character profiles.

She started reading. It took her about five minutes to realize she had stumbled into dangerous territory. At the same moment, a red alert flashed across her screen: *I'm being tracked.*

"Damn it!" she cursed, yanking the power cord from the socket.

She was well aware that such data was protected by every possible security measure. One of them was an immediate alert notifying the relevant security services that an unauthorized person was accessing the content. If she had only used her company's computer, it might not have been a problem. But driven by curiosity, she had used her private machine.

The next day, right on schedule, grim men in black suits showed up at her apartment and her workplace, confiscating all her equipment. The interrogations, the questioning, and the nitpicking over every detail began.

A month later, she received her first summons to court for a criminal case brought against her by an overzealous prosecutor. Unaware of the severity of what she was facing, she began educating herself online, searching for information about the charges. It was serious. *Too serious,* she thought.

For her first hearing, she requested a public defender, as she couldn't afford a lawyer. The court, considering her financial situation and the fact she was still a student, granted her request.

That was when she met *him*—Piotr was assigned as her public defender. He masterfully proved that she was guilty of nothing and had merely been carrying out the orders given to her by her boss. If anyone was at fault, it was the WSI personnel responsible for the ineffective destruction of the hard drives. The prosecutor had been demanding a one-year prison sentence; any conviction would have ruined her life.

She was grateful to him, but not enough to go to bed with him. At first, he made a few advances, which she found terribly amusing, but he was too old for her taste at the time—she wasn't into guys like him.

When she turned him down, he backed off gracefully. To her surprise, however, their acquaintance continued.

He called her two months later, just after she learned she had been accepted to university. She was on the verge of declining the offer and switching to part-time studies, but that phone call changed everything.

"Aśka, come to my office," she heard.

"You have an office?" she asked, surprised. She knew he worked for one of the many law firms in the city.

He gave her the address, and they arranged to meet the next day. Curious about what he could possibly want, she went to the meeting. She entered the office building, went up to the second floor, and found two empty rooms, a hallway, and a restroom.

And there he was, sitting in a chair and smiling contentedly.

"Come in. Welcome to my office," he said, a smile on his face.

"And where, exactly, do you see an office here?" she asked.

"It will be. Just a few more days," he assured her. "So, how are you? I heard you got into university."

"Yes, but I can't afford it."

"You don't have to. I wanted to meet you about that."

She looked at him in surprise. He could be very annoying with those all-seeing eyes of his, which were now gazing at her with clear satisfaction.

He walked over to the windowsill, where a briefcase was lying. He picked it up and walked toward her.

"I have a proposal for you."

She waited to hear what he would say next.

But instead, he took her by the hand, saying, "I'm taking you to dinner. We'll discuss the rest there."

He knew that sometimes there wasn't enough food at her home. He had once dropped by her small, modestly furnished apartment unannounced. They were just eating dinner, if you could call the meager offering on the table a dinner. She had scolded him sharply for showing up without warning. She was ashamed, quite unnecessarily, as there was no abundance at his place either—a fact he had made perfectly clear to her then.

As they sat in a nearby restaurant, he laid out his proposal.

"I have a job for you. You will study, and I will pay for your tuition and living expenses. In exchange, you will do some freelance work for me during your studies," he added. "After you graduate, you'll be obligated to work for my company for two years. Does such an arrangement suit you?"

"Are there any hidden clauses?" she asked. "I don't want to be a student who's an escort girl in exchange for tuition and rent."

"There are no other, immoral, clauses," he assured her. "You will be my investment for the future."

"In the first year, you'll receive two thousand złotys per month. That's what I can afford for now, plus extra pay for every job you take on," he explained.

"And your university grades must be as high as possible. I've reserved the right to check your transcript—it's in the contract," he added.

Then she understood he wasn't joking.

"Okay, I agree," she said quickly, stunned by the offer. "Or maybe you want to *buy* me?" she tested him, thinking that if that were the case, it wasn't worth it.

"Of course I want to buy you," he replied. "But not your body—your intellect. I believe in you, and I believe this will pay off for my company."

She was so happy signing the papers that she kissed him on both cheeks.

"You have me at your disposal," she said, then added after a moment, "My intellect, of course."

She believed him then and never regretted it. She never betrayed him or moved to another company, despite many tempting offers. Now that they had climbed to the top of the intelligence industry, they no longer had to look for clients; they could choose the most interesting cases.

She had an unwritten agreement with Piotr. He decided which cases they took, and she, with her journalistic contacts, vetted their clients.

"We can't take everything that comes our way. Some things are so rotten we'd never get out of the cesspool for the rest of our lives, and then some," he explained, justifying why he rejected certain orders involving Themis and the legal profession. "The corruption, nepotism, and cronyism there are so deeply entrenched it would take an earthquake to root them out. Or, as my friend used to say, a second Stalin."

"What did they do to him?" she had wondered back then. Now she knew he was right, and she never again questioned his judgment on individual orders.

"I've been verifying Joanna's story," Aśka said to Piotr a few days later. "So far, everything checks out. The train crash and her parents' deaths are true; that's all publicly available information. Her personal data is classified in the government offices, but that's not a problem for me. I already have everything I need; I didn't even need to hack in anywhere. She's extremely clean, especially considering her place on the Forbes list," Aśka reported.

They were sitting with Piotr in a "clean room"—a windowless space with double doors—discussing their client's situation.

Piotr listened distractedly; he was thinking about how to tell Aśka about his changing relationship with Joanna. He couldn't keep it from her. Aśka was his accomplice and friend. Though much younger, he had always treated her with respect, sometimes with a slight, patronizing air. Only after discovering how sharp and accurate her observations and findings were did he gain the proper perspective and stop overseeing her, trusting her completely.

She quickly realized this and did everything not to disappoint him. Sometimes she was a little irresponsible in her computer activities, but he knew nothing about that. He used a computer for notes, writing, and general matters. For her, the computer was a passion, a hobby, and it held no secrets from her.

She had once told him, "If I didn't work with you, I'd be a programmer, and in my free time—a hobbyist hacker." At every step, she proved she was a top-tier specialist, which he had known perfectly well from the start of their acquaintance.

"Aśka, I wanted to tell you something before you find out for yourself," he began cautiously.

"Go on. It's obvious to anyone how you two look at each other."

"Is it that obvious?" he was surprised.

"You're the only man who has appeared at her private house in five years, and in her apartment in the office building in three. That's verified information from her security detail. I had a chat with someone who's worked for her for a long time," she added.

"You know all this?"

"I do. But it doesn't change anything—not between us, and not in this job. Right?" she asked.

"Of course. Except for the fact that I've decided to equalize our shares to a 50/50 split because of this case. You've earned it."

"Thanks. I'll put that toward donuts," she said. That was her style, and he liked her for it.

"I checked the police files," she continued, speaking unhurriedly. "I looked two years back and two years forward from the date of the assault. I went through newspapers, police blotters, hospitals—everywhere there could be information about rapes from that period. I was looking for the same or similar modus operandi. I found nothing. My informant checked the National Police Headquarters database, where they keep central records and statistics on all solved and unsolved rape cases in Poland."

When she said "my informant," Piotr never knew if she meant herself or if she had actually gotten the information from someone else. But they were already deep into the case, so he remained silent and listened.

"The 'in a van' method hasn't been repeated anywhere else. Yes, there were rapes in vehicles, but the perpetrator and victim knew each other, and the victim got in willingly."

"What's your theory?" he asked.

"I think they acted impulsively. An opportunity presented itself, so they took it."

"I don't think so. It doesn't add up for me—the silence, the bag. Rapists, especially in a group, usually try to establish some contact with the victim, sometimes with fatal results. Here, the bag over the head clearly indicates they didn't want to cause her any *other* harm. In my opinion, it was a deliberate action. I just don't know the motive. She was a snot-nosed seventeen-year-old. What could she have done to anyone?" Aśka wondered.

"She might not have done anything to anyone," Piotr interjected. "Maybe the guys just wanted to have fun?" he speculated.

"And they were just driving around with a sack in the van, looking for a random victim? No, that doesn't make sense," Aśka insisted on her version.

Piotr would have preferred it to be a random event, but he didn't believe it himself, not with the DHL packages contradicting that theory.

"What about the packages sent to her?" he asked.

"I didn't find anything. They were sent from a DHL office; no one remembers anything, and the sender's address doesn't exist."

"The photos?"

"Standard—printed on an HP color printer. There are thousands of them in the city."

"The people, the background in the photos, the places they were taken?" he continued.

"This is where it gets interesting. Joanna accurately identified the place and time they were taken. She checked everything herself and gave us the information. There was only one thing she couldn't do."

"Namely?"

"She doesn't recognize anyone in the photos. She claims she doesn't know these people."

"I can believe that," Piotr said, defending her.

"But I know almost everything about one of them. I wrote my own program after hours," she added, laughing, "and I used it to scan social networks. I found one of them on Facebook."

"Who is it?"

"A former special services agent—currently a Director of one of the divisions in Joanna's company. A fairly important figure."

"Is it possible she doesn't know him?"

"She may have seen him, but to her, he was just a pawn. She might not have remembered him," Aśka said confidently. "There are dozens of people like that in her company."

"And how many of them are former agents?" he asked.

"Good question. Should we find out?"

"But that's not all," she said. "Do you know what else I did and what I discovered?"

No, he didn't know, and he didn't want to know *how* she did it, but he asked, "What?"

"Yesterday morning, I planted a tiny device in his house, a townhouse in Witomin. I didn't even have to go inside; the wiring runs overhead, and his receiver-transmitter antenna sticks out the window. When he turns on his computer, he logs in, and at the same time at my place. Then I have access to his computer. He even brings his laptop to work. So confident, or so stupid. He logs into the company server and copies the data he's interested in, then transfers it all to his home computer. He uses the same password for everything. But that's not all. The guy sends the data directly to Senator G... at his company in Warsaw."

"A spy," Piotr concluded. "What do you want to catch him for?"

"For a major scandal. It could threaten Joanna's entire company."

"What are we going to do about it?" Piotr asked.

"Nothing for now—we keep investigating. But from now on, be very careful. Not all former Military Intelligence agents are stupid enough to post their photos online," Piotr warned her.

"Where there's one, there are others. We have to catch them all, one by one. Even though our original job wasn't to uncover corporate espionage, we'll do it for Joanna. Somehow, this is all connected to our case, and I'll handle it personally," Piotr declared.

"I'm leaving the work on Senator G... to you. Act with the utmost caution. Don't involve anyone else, and don't commission anyone to take action against him or to gather information about him. You have a free hand in your methods regarding G... You have the green light. Work decisively and quickly."

"I've already had dealings with this gentleman from my time at the law firm. I don't know him personally, but I know enough from the two cases I handled to learn the methods he uses."

"Tell me about it," she asked.

He settled into his chair and began, a hint of uncertainty in his voice betraying his inner struggle before recounting his first major courtroom defeat. Back then, he still believed in the courts, in justice—those naive, youthful ideas about the world and his future career. It was that case that stripped him of his confidence and the feeling that his work was what he had dreamed of when he went to law school. Every shred of hope was torn from him; every particle of trust he had placed in the system was shattered. His faith in a blind Lady Justice was skinned raw, and he realized that the justice he was dealing with was just business like any other, only dressed in clichés and covered with a black judicial robe.

"I won't go into all the details; it would take too long. So, I'll tell you briefly what happened to me then."

"I remember one afternoon, a client came to the law firm where I was the junior lawyer on duty. In short, he was a novice entrepreneur trying his hand at business, one of the many springing up in the young capitalist market of the early nineties."

"The wholesale company he founded was developing, gaining more and more customers. But back then, the efficiency of our authorities was, to put it mildly, not great."

"This guy—let's call him the Client—was visited once a month in his warehouse by steroid-pumped thugs offering him 'protection' against thieves and, as they put it, 'unexpected fires' or theft of his vans. Their arguments were persuasive; before each visit, he'd find the tires on his vans slashed. As his warehouse grew, so did the 'protection' money these 'bodyguards' demanded. His reports to the police were met with smug smiles and helpless shrugs."

"Instead of tackling the gang, he received useless advice from the police: 'Install cameras, buy dogs,' and other nonsense."

"When their demands exceeded his finances and he refused to pay, he was assaulted in front of his own house, taken to his warehouse, and beaten. They threatened his family, trying to force him to sign two blank promissory notes. When he still refused, they showed him a fabricated invoice claiming he owed them a large sum. They then took him to his bank and forced him to write a check, cleaning out his account."

"How is that possible? At the bank?" Aśka interrupted him, looking up from the blank notepad where she had yet to write a single thing. Nothing Piotr had said so far had seemed worth noting.

"Yes, unfortunately. Back then, thugs weren't afraid of anything because the police were weak and inept. At least that unit was. But as if that wasn't enough, they announced they'd be back in a week."

"The client reported the incident in person to the Provincial Police Headquarters, hoping they would take it seriously. They did, and when the thugs returned for more money, they were arrested. They were charged, the case went to court, and I represented the wholesaler."

"Their defense attorney was a former prosecutor who knew all the tricks for using false documents and evidence. Together with his wife, also a lawyer, they submitted a pile of forged documents to the court and called witnesses who weren't worth a damn. But that wasn't all. The original invoice they claimed proved my client's debt mysteriously disappeared from the court records. Pretending to be disappointed, they presented the court with a certified copy from a friendly notary—all to prevent a graphological analysis of the signatures on the 'original' invoices. Then came other false evidence: clumsily edited audio recordings. These tapes shouldn't have been admitted as evidence at all, as they were supposed to be a recording of the extortion but had all of my client's denials edited out."

"Yet, the court accepted this evidence and acquitted the thugs, who didn't hesitate to mock me in the hallway with a finger-gun gesture. I didn't know if it was meant for me or my client standing next to me."

"I later analyzed why it happened. There's only one answer: money. If you have enough of it, even a shady client can arrange everything within the legal system, including winning in court."

"I believe the system is to blame, and the lack of hard rules in the law. Giving judges the discretion to verify evidence is a flawed concept that creates opportunities for mistakes, abuse, and corruption. How is a judge, raised in a greenhouse, surrounded by the same values as their parents, supposed to know about business, the methods of evidence falsification, or the real problems of people left to fend for themselves against criminals? They, having barely skimmed psychology, rush to judge others, unprepared to confront someone who knows the specifics of their work and how to exploit it—like that former prosecutor."

"In obvious cases like burglaries or assaults where the perpetrators are caught red-handed, guilt is clear, and they only decide the sentence. They aren't afraid, protected by immunity, and can resign at any time with a fixed pension, even after just two years on the bench."

"One judge became the laughingstock of the bar and law students after convicting a man for stealing his own share— half a frying pan and two pots—from the kitchen he once shared with his ex-wife. They were divorced and had a property division case. The ex-wife had given the items to her mother, and when the man was visiting, he took them back. To make it funnier, it was the mother-in-law who accused him of theft and won. I ask you—where is the common sense? It's absent in some members of the judiciary, and not just them."

"According to the verdict, he robbed himself and was convicted for it. This trivial matter—though not for him— shows the kind of judges we have. I wondered if he shouldn't have counter-sued his ex-wife, since the pots were now with her, meaning she had also stolen his half of the shared property."

"That's what's called having privileges!" he muttered to himself.

"This story is a warning for you—not everyone in a robe is a decent person. So be careful when you take on a Senator."

He sighed heavily and dragged himself off the couch.

"Get me a strong coffee with a shot of cognac now," he asked.

Aśka thought about everything Piotr had told her. She hadn't expected such a conclusion. Although she had also encountered the injustice and overzealousness of the state authorities firsthand, she had come out of it unscathed. *Yes— but only thanks to Piotr. What if it had been a different lawyer?*

She pushed away the gloomy thoughts. *He is a lawyer; I am an investigator. I have a duty to keep an eye on the powerful and inform society.* Her position in the company was strong; she felt confident enough to face this Mr. G...

"I have an advantage over him," she thought. "I can ask Joanna for help."

She worked for two whole days on this case alone, and when she was ready, she decided to act.

Reading the intelligence report, she stared at the photos pinned to the board, her emotions bubbling inside her. On the right side was a photo of "The Dog"—the former policeman following Joanna.

She numbered the photos:

...Photo No. 1.

A circle around his head and the label: "The Dog."

The tail following Joanna had been tracked since the day Joanna ran that small circle on the Boulevard at Piotr's request. Since then, he hadn't been allowed out of their sight. Four of Aśka's employees took turns following him around the clock.

Apart from that appointed day, he never once drove in the direction of the Boulevard.

How does The Dog know when SHE is going to run? Besides that, Aśka had no idea who he worked for. So far, his movements hadn't indicated any contact with a handler, though she had no doubt one existed.

Only one thing in the report gave her pause: his visit on a Saturday evening to the "LUCKY" restaurant on the outskirts of the city. The large, sprawling villa hid a thinly disguised brothel—officially an escort agency. The stylish restaurant on the ground floor was popular, especially on Fridays and Saturdays. An interesting program, live music, karaoke, and discounts for regulars were the manager's doing. Pretty, approachable girls at the bar tables were a magnet for the wealthiest patrons.

Upstairs were rooms for rent—by the hour. The girls were successful, both those sitting at the tables and those picked up on the spot. The report mentioned his visit but only in a marginal note. He came and left in his own car, so he likely didn't drink. The report didn't answer her main question:

Who did he meet there? The detectives following him hadn't gone inside for fear of being made.

I should check what The Dog was doing there, she concluded. I'll assign someone to follow him there next time. It would be even better if they waited for him inside.

She instructed a young operative to be at the Lucky Restaurant every Friday and Saturday, equipped with a hidden camera and a camera disguised as a lighter.

"And don't forget to buy cigarettes," she reminded him, knowing he didn't smoke.

...Photo No. 2.

She placed these on the left side of the board, circling one head in red and writing next to it: "WSI – NJ." She drew a red line from this circle to a photo of the Senator downloaded from the internet, labeled "Senator G..."

Below were two photos sent to Joanna by the mysterious sender, taken at parties where Joanna was with several people.

It took her less than half a day to identify the names and positions of the ministry employees, security, and staff. All she had to do was visit the appropriate websites where their CVs and photos were publicly available. She lost interest in these people once she was sure they were unrelated to the case.

...Photo No. 3

Three circles and one label: "Operation."

Afterwards.

Two circles and "???" for each.

...Photo No. 4

Two circles and the label: "Ministry Employee."

One circle – "Security."

One circle - "???"

Second circle - "???"

She still had four identities left to discover.

After a moment's hesitation, she called Joanna.

"You have a spy, or a camera on you," she said calmly.

"Do you know who it is or where the camera is?" Joanna asked, her tone factual.

"Not yet, but there's a way to find out."

"How?"

"Will you be at your residence tomorrow morning?"

"Yes."

"Then don't tell anyone—not security, not the staff. Tomorrow morning, put on a tracksuit as if you're going for a run on the Boulevard. Get in your car at exactly ten o'clock. Drive a few kilometers from the gate, then change your mind. But don't return to the mansion for at least two or three hours."

"Can you do it? Do you have the time?"

"Consider it done. I'm here to help you," Joanna declared her willingness to participate.

Aśka knew that if the camera was active, the information would reach The Dog. He would see her leave and head to the Boulevard to wait for her. If he was just an informant, he would leave and return quickly once he realized she wasn't coming.

At exactly ten o'clock, The Dog jumped into his car and headed for the Boulevard. He had plenty of time. He wanted to finally find out who SHE was meeting there. He'd seen her running with some guy before.

He waited for an hour—she never showed. *She changed her plans,* he thought, and drove home. *No photos today. The boss won't be happy.* He knew "Pikuś" could get nasty. But that wasn't what scared him most. There had been nothing on her for two weeks. If this continued, Pikuś would cut off his cash flow, and it was a decent amount.

Lately, he'd been wondering if it would be better to go to her directly. She'd probably want to know why he was following her. He himself had no idea, but he knew what kind of people he was dealing with, especially Pikuś, who had recruited him. *The stupid punk thinks he's smarter than me. It never occurred to him I could follow him, too.*

He had taken on this Pikuś as a threat after discovering he was demanding more and more money while showing little interest in the actual job of tailing the head of DLACOM.

It wasn't hard to follow Pikuś—the loner spent most of his time at home, his social life limited to two or three pubs in the evening.

First, he discovered Pikuś's connection to a certain escort agency run by a woman named "Zdzira." It turned out she was a good friend of Pikuś.

Just a low-life, he thought as he chatted with a girl at the bar in her restaurant. That's when he met the Boss herself.

"I'm from the police," he introduced himself to the Boss. "Well, I was," he added, seeing the grimace that discouraged conversation. "Now I'm a freelancer, a friend of Pikuś. I work for him," he explained, trying to win her over. After that, it went smoothly.

"You're a nice lady," he said, flattering her, his eyes drilling into her. It wasn't a sophisticated style, but the compliments worked in that atmosphere.

He liked the restaurant and its Boss. He started visiting more often, just for chat and a few drinks. Once, after a few rounds with her, he made a pass—she jokingly pushed him away.

"You see that guy over there? 'Lalusia'? He's mine, so stop, or he'll rearrange your face. If you need relief, take one of these girls," she added, pointing to three pretty young things on bar stools.

He always used the services of one of the non-Polish girls working there for free, knowing they were there illegally.

He'd sit at the bar, down a quick drink, and signal to Zdzira what he wanted. "Put it on my tab," he'd say. Of course, he never paid.

This continued until Zdzira asked Pikuś, "When is your guy going to pay for the girls?"

That's when Pikuś started threatening him again, so he started tailing Pikuś in retaliation.

He followed him for a whole month until, one day, Pikuś took a taxi to the Gdynia train station for a trip to Warsaw. He followed. At Central Station, he almost lost him, having to keep his distance to avoid being spotted.

When Pikuś entered a large office building near the station and went to the 16th floor, he followed in the next elevator. He didn't see which office Pikuś entered, but it didn't matter—the entire 16th floor and more was occupied by Senator G...'s company.

He waited patiently downstairs for Pikuś to emerge.

Pikuś came out, but not alone—he was with Senator G..., known from TV. Seeing this, he almost choked with excitement. Pretending to be on the phone, he snapped a few photos. When the Senator got into a waiting limousine and left Pikuś on the sidewalk, he knew he had stumbled onto something big. *Now they're really paying me,* he thought happily.

He returned to Gdynia on a different train, thinking the whole way about what a small-time gangster like Pikuś had to do with a Senator. *Why does the Senator receive a shady guy like Pikuś in his office?* The thought nagged at him.

There was also the other guy he'd seen in the corridor on the 16th floor when Pikuś entered a room. He didn't know who he was yet, but he would find out. He still had a few buddies in the police. His only regret was not having time to photograph him; it would have made identification easier.

When he uploaded the Warsaw photos to his computer and saw Pikuś next to Senator G..., he was stunned. *What do these three have in common?* He was sure the guy from the corridor had led Pikuś to the Senator. *I need to find a way to contact the head of DLACOM.* So far, she'd been unreachable; her security wouldn't let him get near.

He decided to send her a letter with the photos he'd taken of her, requesting a meeting on an important matter.

He sat down at his computer and wrote.

"Madam!" Aśka read on her computer.

By the time she finished, she knew The Dog was just a pawn, a tracker who knew nothing. He knew less than she did.

He sent the letter but never made it to the proposed meeting.

Unfortunately for him, when he took the photos in Warsaw, he used the same cell phone that received the feed from the camera hidden on the head of DLACOM's gate.

As soon as he connected his phone to his computer, Aśka gained complete access to all its data. She could even alter the contents without him noticing.

At noon, when her operatives reported The Dog's fruitless wait on the Boulevard, she decided to act. It was time to tell Joanna everything and let her decide the next steps. She had to do it; it was her safety at stake. Piotr wasn't there; he'd gone to Warsaw to do some sniffing around himself.

She grabbed the phone and dialed Joanna's number. The line rang four times before she answered.

Aśka knew Joanna had seen the caller ID. "Yes, Aśka, I'm sorry to keep you waiting. I can talk now."

Always polite and tactful, Aśka thought. She admired Joanna's achievements but didn't envy her.

"I have very important news. Piotr isn't here; he's in Warsaw. When can we talk?"

Joanna had been briefed by Piotr about Aśka's competence. She knew she wouldn't call without good reason.

"Alright, come to my house at seven tonight," she said politely.

"I'll be there," Aśka confirmed briefly and hung up.

Now I have some time, Aśka thought. She went into her office, which housed her personal computer. As the head of the intelligence agency and an investigator, she had given herself this essential tool. It cost a fortune, but Piotr had accepted the bill without question. The hardware was just the beginning; all the software, secure internet access, server security, and independent power and cabling made it impenetrable to any intruder. The security services wouldn't be able to track her like they had before.

The walls, ceiling, and floor of her office were soundproofed and lined with a special magnetic mesh. At the push of a button—or automatically if the system detected a breach—it would activate, emitting jamming waves. During a test, Aśka had disrupted every computer in the building. The windows, coated with a special film, prevented eavesdropping via laser microphones. From the inside, they looked normal, but from the outside, no one could see in. They also blocked infrared and night-vision imaging. No paparazzi could get a shot through them.

Piotr had shaken his head in admiration when he read about all the security measures, but he'd groaned when he saw the cost.

"Why do we need all this?" he'd asked.

"We've reached the highest level in our field. We need the proper equipment to match," she'd replied.

"Well, as always, you're right," he'd conceded.

Now, Aśka could finally deal with Mr. G... in her own way. I have a free hand. Piotr won't ask me how I know what I know.

"I have a journalistic duty to protect my sources, even when the source is me," she had once explained when he pressed her for information.

"From a legal standpoint, I'm not entirely convinced you're right," he'd argued.

She made herself a coffee and told the secretary she was unavailable except for calls from Piotr or someone from DLACOM. She settled comfortably into her chair. She had time until five, then she needed to go home and get ready to visit Joanna. *What the hell do I buy for her?* she wondered for a moment. She had no idea what you bring to someone like Joanna on a first visit to her home.

"Mrs. Lolo," she asked, entering the secretariat, "what do you buy for someone when you go to their house for the first time?"

"Is it family? A friend?"

More of a business associate," Aśka replied.

"Nothing," the secretary said. "A gift creates an obligation. Unless it's a woman, then flowers are always fine."

"Then I'll get some nice flowers for the lady. I'll pick them up on my way."

"What kind?"

"I don't know—you decide."

Aśka drove up to the gate of the residence at exactly seven, then slowly rolled toward the wide front door. A maid in a blue apron and a bodyguard in a black suit were waiting for her. She followed the maid into the grand foyer, down a wide corridor, until Joanna appeared at the last door on the left.

They greeted each other quite warmly, with air kisses on the cheeks, before Joanna led her into the living room where she received guests. She offered coffee and cake, which the same young maid brought in.

The interior didn't overwhelm Aśka; she had a certain idea from movies of what the homes of the very rich looked like. She'd always wondered why they needed four bedrooms and eight bathrooms. Her parents' home was modest, and she'd never complained. Sure, she'd recently bought an apartment, but it was on a mortgage, and she was perfectly happy with it.

Joanna was very nice and kind, but she treated Aśka differently than she treated Piotr. Only when she realized Aśka wasn't a romantic rival had her warmth visibly increased. Without ceremony, she had once said to her, "Call me Joanna."

Now, sitting across from Aśka, she asked curiously, "What have you found?"

"I wouldn't call it 'interesting.' It's more like something very dangerous and disturbing that concerns your company, Joanna. I don't yet know what connections it might have to our original case," she added.

"Speak," Joanna said, her tone instantly serious.

Aśka was perfectly prepared. She pulled out a folding display frame and set it up. Then she took a rolled-up board from her bag, unrolled it, and hung it on the frame. Finally, she produced the photographs.

Joanna watched attentively.

On the left side of the board, Aśka pinned four enlarged prints of the photos Joanna had received.

"In this first photograph, from the reception at the Ministry of Treasury," Aśka began in a calm, matter-of-fact tone, circling two figures standing near Joanna, "the first person is your employee, the Head of the Public Procurement Division, who has been with your company for years. The second person is, for now, an unidentified businessman. The third is another one of your employees. Do you know him?" she asked, more as a formality. Aśka had already identified everyone.

But Joanna didn't know him and couldn't figure out why he was there.

"The rest are ministry employees and staff," Aśka continued. "They have nothing to do with this case."

In the second photo, she circled only one figure: the former Military Intelligence agent she had investigated, now a DLACOM employee.

"I'm here because of this gentleman," she said. "He's also your employee, 'NJ,' a former WSI agent. That wouldn't be surprising if it weren't for what he does. I came across his photo online, so I know where he works and what his role is."

On the right, she pinned a photo of The Dog and drew a red line connecting it to the previous photo.

"This one is The Dog—that's his nickname. A former policeman who followed you on the Boulevard and took pictures of you. This one here is 'X'," she said, hanging his photo next to The Dog's and connecting them with a red line. "These two know each other. I believe The Dog was working on X's orders. I don't have his full details yet, but it's a matter of a day or two."

Joanna looked at the photographs in silence.

"Change your security camera operator," Aśka said suddenly.

"You have all the right people."

"Do you know where the camera is installed?" Joanna asked, surprised and irritated.

"Yes, I picked up the signal. The mini-camera is on your main gate, hidden near your official security camera. It activates automatically when the gate opens and deactivates when it closes. A simple method used by the police. The signal is sent via a radio transmitter to a cell phone; I assume it has a short range, but it's enough to know who is visiting you and when you are coming or going."

"He probably also tracked Piotr. I hope he doesn't know who he is," Joanna said to Aśka.

"Don't count on it. Even if he didn't recognize him, he can find out from the license plate. But maybe he's only interested in you."

Joanna fidgeted restlessly but did not interrupt.

"JN, your employee," Aśka tapped his photograph, returning to the main thread, "copies materials from your work server and sends them to Senator G...'s company in Warsaw." She fell silent for a moment, then continued.

"...X is also in contact with Senator G... For reasons I'm still uncovering, The Dog followed X and tracked him to a Renovation Company based in the same office building. There, X met with another individual—let's call him 'Y'—and they both went to see Senator G..."

"The Dog took photos of them with his cell phone—the same phone that receives the feed from the camera on your gate. Because I have access to that phone and his computer, it's clear they all know each other. They all work for Mr. G..."

"As you can see, some of the people in the photos sent to you also appear in The Dog's pictures from Warsaw. This is no coincidence, which is why Piotr went to Warsaw with a team. I believe he will find the man we're looking for there."

This time, she was not wrong. The person they were searching for was identified in a photo taken by Piotr a few days later.

"The Dog wrote you a letter; you'll probably receive it tomorrow. He wants to play both sides and get money from you for his information. But he doesn't know anything that I don't, unless he's stored something else on his computer. The Dog did make a note about the mysterious man he saw with X in the hallway, which is why Piotr went to Warsaw to find him."

"However, we can still use The Dog to our advantage," she added.

"Returning to the case of your employee, the former Military Intelligence agent... where there is one, there are usually more. Those are Piotr's words," she noted.

"I need your help to catch them all," Aśka concluded her brief presentation. She walked back to the table and sat down.

After taking a bite of cake and a sip of tea, she looked attentively at Joanna, who remained silent. After a moment, Aśka continued.

"What I mean is, I *could* find them within your company myself, but I refuse to use the typical methods for uncovering such individuals. It would violate my professional ethics. You are our client, and I will not hack into your internal systems or gather information by bribing your employees."

"Therefore, please assign a trusted IT specialist from your team to work with me. Clearly define their permissions and the scope of systems we can access. With that, I can find everyone quickly and cleanly."

CHAPTER IV
SQUIRT

Pikuś showed up at his office unannounced.

"I told you never to come here," he growled. "You were supposed to leave a message in the 'waiting room'," he said, referring to their designated dead-drop.

"But this is urgent," Pikuś replied.¶"Nothing is so urgent that it can't follow procedure. Military Intelligence doesn't sleep; they have informants everywhere. And after that mess, they could be watching us."

He didn't know how it happened, but a week ago, customs officers had seized 20 kilos of cocaine. The drug shipment, smuggled as usual within a military transport, had gotten stuck at the Gdynia container terminal. A routine inspection with a sniffer dog had detected the drugs in one of the containers. The customs officers were stunned to find it belonged to the army.

The shipping logistics had failed, and instead of arriving in Świnoujście, it was unloaded in Gdynia. This particular shipment had been sent from their repair base in Ghazni, Pakistan—a route he couldn't control. *They must have screwed up something at the base.* Of course, it immediately became a major scandal. It was only thanks to the special services containing the story that it hadn't leaked to the media. But the investigation was ongoing, and no one knew how it would end.

He approached Pikuś, grabbed him by the lapels of his jacket, and slammed him against the wall.

"If you come here again, you won't leave alive," he threatened in a tone that made Pikuś genuinely fear for his life right then and there.

Pikuś hadn't been afraid of him before. He'd been with him from the start, but he lacked the ambition and intelligence to take over their fledgling criminal organization, so he'd become his right-hand man. Of the original four, only he and Zdzira had remained at the same level, a tight-knit group of old buddies.

"Bandit" had grown into a major businessman with a company in Warsaw, and G... had become a senator.

"What do you have?" he asked, cooling down slightly.

"I have to get rid of The Dog. He's useless for tailing the head of DLACOM," Pikuś said, not mentioning that The Dog had ended up at Zdzira's place because he was following *him*.

"The head of DLACOM hired some investigators from Gdynia, but I don't know why. Their boss must have charmed his way to her, because the paparazzi caught them kissing," he boasted, delivering the news.

He sat down in his chair, regaining his composure. "I'm pouring myself a drink."

He stood by the window, thinking intensely. This wasn't entirely new information, though he hadn't known The Dog had visited Zdzira.

Recently, when he'd seen her, they'd had a terrible fight—about money, of course. He'd refused to keep funding her gigolos.

"A restaurant and an agency aren't enough for you now?" he had fumed, calling her an old whore. "How do you manage to burn through it all? You should be paying *me* back!" he'd shouted.

It wasn't that he cared about the money itself, but there had to be order. He also had his own payoffs to make, greasing the palms that helped his business in Afghanistan. The military contacts were greedy hyenas. It was good they didn't know about the drugs, though now, who could say if they didn't suspect him of the smuggling.

"Sorry," he said to Pikuś. "I was upset. But there are cameras everywhere here. Get rid of this Dog. When I come to Gdynia, we'll meet at the usual spot. I'll let you know. And since you're here, we'll go see G... Just for a moment," he added, grabbing the phone. "You'll tell him what you just told me."

An hour later, Bandit returned to his office, and Pikuś left the building with Senator G..., the old friends walking out in unison. They didn't know that at that very moment, The Dog was capturing them on his cell phone.

A few days later, in the same location, Piotr also photographed them. It was then that Piotr and his team of four investigators began tailing Senator G... They followed him for two full days, long enough to identify his contacts and conclude that Senator G... and a bland-looking businessman from the same office building had many friends in high-ranking military circles. Their coordinated visit to the Ministry of Defense gave Piotr a lot to think about.

Senator X and Senator G... know each other, and Pikuś knows X, so maybe all three of them are connected.

He called Aśka from Warsaw.

"Listen, check their backgrounds quickly. See if all three of them are connected—I'm sending you a photo of a bland 'Bandit,' a close associate of Senator G..."

An hour later, he had his answer.

All three of them, except for The Dog, had attended the same school and lived on the same housing estate in Grabówek, Gdynia.

Pikuś was waiting for The Dog at the pre-arranged spot. The same address, the same courtyard, only the walls had aged since their youth. It was here, as boys, that they had discovered a secret entrance to a network of underground tunnels. They hadn't known who built the labyrinth of passages and rooms back then. Now he knew it was constructed just before the war; the tunnels originated from a pre-war transport troop garrison quite a distance away.

The defense system, designed for the rapid movement of sabotage units, was meant to destabilize German troops in the event of war.

The tunnels, partially destroyed by the fighting, had been an attractive haunt in their youth, used for meetings and stashing stolen goods. Now, they would be used to get rid of The Dog.

"What took you so long? You think I have nothing better to do than wait for you?" he spat angrily as The Dog got out of his car.

He stood in the shadow of a dilapidated wall next to a large gate that led directly to their secret entrance.

"Got lost," The Dog said apologetically, looking suspiciously at his surroundings. He wasn't afraid of Pikuś; he was physically stronger, and his hand-to-hand combat training made him overconfident. He looked disdainfully at Pikuś's protruding gut and added, "What do you want?"

"I have a new job for you. Pays well," Pikuś said, knowing this would lull The Dog's vigilance.

"Yeah? What's it about?" The Dog asked, interested.

"You'll see. We're going. I'll show you a video of who you're supposed to follow."

He turned away from The Dog and walked towards the gate. He covered the ten steps to the shadowy entrance with a calm stride, not looking back at The Dog following him.

The Dog didn't reply, lost in thought. A video? Why a video? What's this about?

Preoccupied, he didn't notice Pikuś had vanished from his sight. He followed him into the gateway, and the darkness there kept him from seeing Pikuś pressed flat against the wall. It was too late when he glimpsed a long object swinging toward his head from his peripheral vision. There was a soft, sickening crack of a skull fracturing, and his consciousness didn't even register the long dagger that pierced his heart immediately after.

His body went limp and slumped to the ground.

Pikuś bent down, grabbed The Dog's legs, and dragged the motionless body. It was a struggle, but he managed to haul it the five meters to the open metal flap at the base of the wall, beyond which a dark, oblong opening was visible. He shoved the corpse into the depths of the pit, then climbed in after it, closing the flap behind him. A dozen steps below, The Dog lay in a strangely contorted position. Blood from his shattered head slowly spread in a dark red stain across the concrete floor.

"Damn it," Pikuś cursed. "This is going to make a mess."

He approached the body, pulled on leather gloves, and rifled through all the pockets, throwing the contents into a bag he'd brought. He left only the car keys and registration in the wallet. Once he'd finished searching, he calmly stepped back outside, closed the metal flap, and secured it with a large padlock through its steel loops. He put the key in his left jacket pocket, got into his car, started the engine, and drove towards the parking lot on the Boulevard, where he decided to abandon The Dog's vehicle. He didn't see that four keen eyes had carefully observed his every move.

After ditching the car, he headed to Zdzira's, intending to have some fun and forget what he'd done an hour earlier. He was exhausted, and only the promise of alcohol and sex could make his evening pleasant, erasing the moments of fear that had gripped him as he dragged the dead body. It was the only time a late passerby could have spotted him.

The villa where his best and only friend worked was located near the on-ramp to the city ring road. From the street, it was set back by a small parking square. In front, a row of large glass windows hinted at its purpose, and any possible doubt was erased by the large, ever-glowing red neon sign above them: LUCKY RESTAURANT.

A wide entrance with double doors was separated from the parking lot by three tiled concrete steps. Walking around the side of the building, one would find a tall metal fence attached to the wall, with a small gate and a buzzer instead of a handle. Pikuś used this entrance, buzzing in the agreed-upon pattern. Entering the back, he came into a large garden. A second, single-story building was attached to the rear of the villa, housing Zdzira's private apartments. Only a select few were allowed past the threshold of this part of the house. Passing through a servant's room manned by two security guards, he entered her domain, walking straight into her office.

He looked around anxiously before speaking. "Why's it so empty today? No cars in the lot."

"It's too early for the business crowd. You'll see in a few hours," she replied from her chair, not even bothering to stand up. She had watched his approach on the monitor from the moment he drove in, frowning and squinting ridiculously without her glasses, which she refused to wear. "They age me," she'd say, "and contact lenses are too much trouble."

"Got any new goods?" he asked.

She didn't need to ask what he meant. "Two were brought from Ukraine yesterday by the couriers. But they're not... broken in yet."

"Fine, give me one. I'll break her in," he assured her.

She knew he was capable of it. In a way, it was to her advantage. She didn't consider herself a madam or a trafficker. She constantly emphasized that she was a businesswoman; it was just chance that she ran an escort agency and not some other venture.

All these years, she had been consumed by envy and rage towards Bandit and Senator G... She only tolerated Pikuś because she considered him beneath her in her personal hierarchy.

She watched as he got up and went to the liquor cabinet. He poured half a glass of whiskey and downed it in one gulp. He returned and slumped heavily into the chair.

It was then she realized Pikuś was uneasy, that something was weighing on him.

"Alright, go on. I'll be downstairs later," she said, pressing a hidden button under her desk.

The girl who entered knew Pikuś and his role in the business. "Take him to the new one," Zdzira instructed.

Without a word, he followed the girl through the corridor connecting her private quarters to the hotel and restaurant section. On the stairs, he trailed behind her, staring at her legs. They went up two floors to the attic where the "new" girls were kept. She unlocked a door at the end of the hall with a key she kept in her bra and let him in.

Inside, Pikuś scanned the room. The girl sitting on the bed was very young, maybe seventeen or eighteen. She looked at him with terrified eyes.

"Undress," he barked at her in broken Russian.

"What do you want?" she said in a tearful voice, her face a mask of fear.

"We can do this with or without pain," he added in Polish, moving toward her. He grabbed her by the hair and yanked her from the bed onto the floor. He tugged at her blouse, tearing it, and her snow-white breasts spilled out of her bra.

She screamed, a high-pitched, panicked shriek.

He punched her in the face until her head snapped back and her body went limp on the floor.

He hadn't wanted that; he didn't like it when they were unconscious. He hauled her up and threw her onto the bed. He tore off her pants and everything else. Undressing himself, he sat down next to her, waiting for her to come to.

She slowly opened her eyes. Seeing him naked and leaning over her, she didn't resist anymore. She knew how this would end. She clenched her teeth, squeezed her eyes shut, and a muffled sob escaped her throat.

Meanwhile, Zdzira left her office and stepped outside. She had the keys to the car Pikuś had carelessly left on her desk. It wasn't the first time she'd done this; whenever he got drunk, she went through his things. This time, however, what she found horrified her.

He killed him! Otherwise, he wouldn't have The Dog's personal effects. She came to this conclusion while looking through the items in the bag.

She knew The Dog and knew he'd been tailing the head of DLACOM. She'd even done a background check on him when he'd played around with one of her girls. She felt she was on very dangerous ground. She thought about the argument, or rather the screaming match, with Bandit that had led her to send the envelope with the coral beads to the head of DLACOM. She'd been so angry she hadn't been thinking rationally. The desire for revenge had been festering for a long time, ever since she realized her former lover had sidelined her. He surrounded himself with younger, more beautiful women, leaving her in this house to run their first, now seemingly small-time, business.

She entered the restaurant, sat down at a service table, and waited. She wasn't worried anymore. She knew that if she played her cards right, a chest full of money would open for her. And she was starting to need it. The constant rotation of young lovers she surrounded herself with was costing a fortune, and plastic surgery wasn't cheap either. She sat at the bar, slowly sipping red wine. After an hour, Pikuś sat down next to her and ordered dinner.

"Bandit is coming soon," he said to her, talking with his mouth full.

"So what?"

"Nothing. He'll probably want to talk to you about a certain woman."

"Which one?" she pretended not to know.

"Well, you know. His and supposedly *your* daughter."

"What's it to you?" she bristled immediately. She wasn't completely talentless; she understood Bandit was playing a game, but she would defend this girl with everything she had. Beata was her only true love, even if the beginning had been difficult.

Years ago, Bandit had come to her with a little, pretty girl, telling her, "This is your daughter, Beata. Take care of her." He handed her the adoption papers and said in a hard voice, "You are to provide her with a real home and look after her. You will never know poverty again."

"Just like I was, I suppose? *Your* daughter?" she had thrown back angrily. Then she composed herself and asked quietly, "Who is her mother?"

"You. The adoptive one," he added.

"How... what do you mean?" she asked, surprised.

He wasn't in a hurry to answer. "Here are the documents. The notarized deed for this house and the land it's on. It's in Beata's name, and you are the legal custodian of the property until she turns 25. Understood?"

"Yes, I understand. But who did you have the child with?" she dared to ask again, as she hadn't heard of any of his girls getting pregnant by him.

"Her mother is dead. You don't need to know anything else." He ended the conversation and left, leaving her in boundless astonishment and complete confusion. She didn't oppose it. They hadn't been together for over a year, so she had no hold over him, and what he offered in return took her completely by surprise.

She looked at the little blonde girl standing in the corner of the room. Something inside her twitched, a vague memory surfacing. Something she had long forgotten. She looked again. *Yes, she reminds me of... me. I also stood like that in my stepfather's new house, looking fearfully into the eyes of my new 'dad.'*

It took her a long time to learn the role of a mother, but when little Beata gave her the selfless, pure love of a child, she surrendered to that feeling completely. Beata quickly forgot she wasn't her biological mother.

Now Beata was an adult and had been living in London for several years. Secretly from Bandit, Zdzira had bought her an apartment there. When she missed her too much, she would visit.

Beata never found out who her adoptive father was or who her real parents were. Zdzira herself knew little more, and

Bandit never spoke of it again. But she knew he was watching, keeping tabs on Beata from a distance.

That's why she was surprised Pikuś knew so much about it. But she shouldn't have been. Pikuś had been with them from the beginning, and Bandit used him for many things— probably for this, too, she thought as she watched him eat.

"Byczek was here a few days ago. I wouldn't have recognized him, but he reminded me of the old days," she said.

"What did he want?"

"Nothing. He told me about a strange meeting."

"Which one?"

"He was at some company where they asked him questions about the old days and showed him photos."

"'I didn't tell them anything,' he assured me, but he was too insistent. I didn't believe him."

"What company?"

"He didn't want to say. Maybe he's trying to pull something. Look into it," she added.

"Where can I find him?"

"He said he often hangs out at the Beer Hall by the Gdynia train station."

"Fine. I'll pay him a visit."

They said goodbye like old friends who had run out of things to say to each other.

Zdzira sighed heavily, got up, and went to her room. She looked at the desk and the photo of Beata standing there.

Something is happening around this case. Maybe it's because of those coral beads. She began to regret sending them. Those photos were a mistake. She became acutely aware that Byczek had been with the head of DLACOM.

She began pacing the room nervously. I'll call Beata, she decided. I need to find out if she's noticed anything suspicious around her. She grabbed the phone.

"Hello, sweetie!" she said, suddenly smiling when she heard Beata's voice.

"Mommy, I'm glad you called! How are you?"

"I'm... worried," she said, suddenly making a decision. "I want to see you. I'm coming right away," she added. "I'll be in London in three days. We need to talk." She said it with a firm determination to tell her the truth. She couldn't do it over the phone.

"I'll be waiting. Call me when your flight lands."

She put down the phone, and a strange calm came over her. *I won't lie to her anymore,* she decided.

As Pikuś had said, Bandit visited her two days later. She had already bought her ticket to London, so his visit made her nervous.

"Pikuś was here," he began, collapsing into the armchair in her office.

"He's always here."

"What about this Byczek?" he asked.

"Nothing. I told Pikuś everything I know."

She was terrified he might guess which company Byczek had been dealing with.

"What the hell is he up to? Do you know anything more?" he asked, watching her carefully.

"No, nothing beyond what he told me. It was probably some kind of scam; he thought he could get money out of me. He looked like a homeless man."

"Fine. I'll look into it and find out what he meant."

Just like with The Dog, she wanted to ask. A spike of fear pierced her. If Byczek was with the head of DLACOM, Bandit can find out about my role in this.

"He was drunk, rambling. His stories are a bluff," she tried to downplay Byczek's visit.

Bandit raised his eyebrows and looked at her with a cold, penetrating gaze.

"Why are you going to see Beata?" he unexpectedly changed the subject.

"I miss her," she replied. "Beata turns 28 in two months. She should have known long ago that this house is her property."

"Do you want to tell her about it?"

"Yes. May I?"

"You may. But not a word about me," he added. "Let everything remain as it was. Anyway, she'll find out everything herself soon."

"Find out what, specifically?"

"It doesn't matter," he dismissed her.

A very unpleasant feeling came over Zdzira. Did he mean he was going to tell her he's her father?

"What do you mean?" she asked, looking him directly in the eye.

"Nothing that concerns you. And now, I'm going to my place," he muttered, a faint smile on his lips. "Business picking up here?" he asked, already in the doorway, turning back to her for a moment.

"Yes," she managed to answer before he disappeared into the hallway.

What the hell about Byczek? she thought intensely, staring at the photograph of Beata on her desk. He can't know anything about the rape. But he didn't just end up at DLACOM by chance. She must have recognized him from the photos I sent her. This has to end; it's getting too dangerous. If Bandit figures it out... I have to send her the rest of the corals with a picture of the van, she decided, resolving to do it as soon as possible.

You didn't have to be a detective to connect the dots. These events were converging, and she had a knack for digging up old secrets. The secret was buried in that adoption, and literally, in the corpse of that ex-cop. *If I find the body before the police do, I'll have leverage over Pikuś and Bandit. Besides, I have to protect Beata. I won't let him drag her into his dirty games.* She made her decision and pressed the button under the desk.

"Send Laluś to me," she spoke into the intercom. All these thoughts had stirred up powerful emotions, and now she wanted to lose herself in Laluś's arms.

I haven't bought him anything in a long time, she thought upon seeing him. Taking his hand, she led him toward the bedroom.

CHAPTER V
ACTION

Joanna sat at the large, oblong conference table in her twelfth-floor office. Before her were neatly arranged folders, some notes, and two active computers. Her gaze swept around the table, not settling on any of the people seated there. She was impatient. Piotr had left unexpectedly for Warsaw two days earlier.

"I have a lead," he had told her. "I'll call as soon as I find out something."

Yesterday morning, she had been busy, and when she finally checked her phone, she saw six missed calls from him. *He has something urgent*, she thought.

She dialed his number from memory, having called him so many times it was etched in her mind.

"What's going on?" she asked.

"I have him!" he said directly, without any preamble.

"Who is it?" she asked, her voice low. The news shook her to her core.

"Not on the phone, believe me. Wait until tomorrow," he pleaded. "I have him in a photo. I don't know the name yet," he explained. "He's definitely in these photos. Maybe you'll recognize him and know his name yourself."

"You can't send me the photo?"

"It's better if I'm there. Your reaction matters. Gather everyone on the list I gave you for tomorrow. I'll be there at eight in the morning and will come straight to you."

She knew all the people on Piotr's list. They were from her social circle from those years.

"Until tomorrow," he said, ending the conversation abruptly.

Now, everyone was sitting and waiting for Piotr. His plane had been delayed by half an hour. She had been so anxious that she sent her helicopter to pick him up from the airport.

"It will be faster," she explained when he objected to this mode of transport.

To her left sat Aga, her cousin and the head of one of her company's divisions. Next to her was Aśka, Piotr's right-hand woman. Then came Robert, a programmer and photo specialist—Aga's former boyfriend, now her husband, and the best professional in Joanna's IT department. Next to him was Henryk, another IT specialist. Finally, "Byczek"—once a bouncer at the "Cicha Piwnica" club—slumped in a chair. *Where did Aśka dig him up so fast?* Joanna wondered for a moment.

Piotr entered without haste, a blissful expression of satisfaction on his face.

"Hello, everyone," he said. He walked around the table and stood before Joanna. He placed three photographs in front of her, then took two steps back and stood behind her, placing a reassuring hand on her shoulder.

"Do you recognize anyone?" he asked, leaning to the side to see her reaction to the photographs.

"I think it's him," she said quietly to Piotr, pointing to one of the figures captured in the photos. "And this is the one Aśka showed me yesterday." She pointed to another man, labeled 'X'.

"I know, she told me. But we don't know who he is yet," he replied.

"Which of you gentlemen is the photo processing specialist?" Piotr asked the room.

"I am," Robert replied.

Piotr approached him, pulling copies of the photographs from his briefcase.

"Please enlarge these photos and make all the people in them look twenty years younger. As soon as possible. We're waiting for the results."

"You can go now," Piotr said to him.

The man looked at Joanna; she was his boss.

"Hurry," she said.

Piotr produced another set of the same photos. "Byczek," he said, addressing the broad-shouldered, tall man who had no idea why this beautiful young woman had paid him so much to be here this morning. He was stunned and overwhelmed by the place. He glanced furtively at the woman sitting at the head of the table; he recognized her face from TV. *What could they possibly want from me?* he had been wondering the whole time.

"Do you recognize any of these people?" Piotr asked, placing the photographs before him.

Joanna lifted her head from the table and waited for his response.

Byczek understood that fate was giving him a chance. He wasn't doing well; he needed a job and wanted to help, but he hadn't brought his reading glasses. He didn't own a pair—he never read anything and couldn't afford an optometrist anyway. The people in the photo blurred into a shapeless spot.

"I... I need a magnifying glass," he dared to say, his voice trembling with emotion.

She gave the order over the phone, and a moment later, a secretary placed a large magnifying glass in front of him.

He took it and brought it close to his eye, leaning over the table to examine one of the photographs. He looked intently for a moment and immediately recognized two people, despite the years that had passed. But he didn't speak; he was thinking. *I could demand cash for this information. But no, better not. There are other people here. If they recognize these bastards, I might not get anything.*

It's them, for sure. He looked at them intently. He'd had some trouble with them back when they used to cause chaos at parties in the "Cicha Piwnica" and other pubs where he worked security.

He picked up the other photos. Two more people in the third photo seemed familiar.

"I know them," he said in a confident voice.

Joanna rose from her chair and walked toward him with quick, nervous steps.

"Speak," she demanded in a tone that sent shivers down his spine.

Looking through the magnifying glass, he pointed a finger at the head of one figure.

"This one is 'Pikuś'."

Aga, sitting at the table, jumped up upon hearing the nickname. She quickly rose and walked over to Byczek.

He repeated the gesture with his finger.

"And this one is his friend. I don't remember his nickname from back then, but now he's Senator G..."

Joanna flinched. She knew that name. Everyone did. However, she controlled herself and asked, "Do you recognize anyone else?"

"Yes, I think I know this woman and the guy next to her, too."

"Try to remember. We'll wait."

The phone on Joanna's desk rang.

"Yes, please send it in quickly," she said into the receiver.

A moment later, the secretary brought in the digitally altered photos.

Joanna took them, and everything became clear. She handed the retouched photos to Byczek.

"Yes, I'm sure now. This one here is 'Zdzira,' the girlfriend of this one," he pointed to another figure, "who they used to call 'Bandit.' That was a long time ago. I don't know what he does now or where he is, but Zdzira supposedly runs some kind of escort agency now."

He looked at the photos a while longer. "I don't know the others. Too many years have passed," he added apologetically.

Aśka looked at Joanna, who gave a slight, almost imperceptible nod.

"You can take him now," Aśka said without a word.

Aśka turned to Byczek. "Thank you. Please keep this all secret. Come to my office tomorrow at noon. We'll discuss your potential usefulness to us and find you something to do."

The secretary escorted him out. Byczek bowed three times, saying, "Goodbye," before disappearing through the door, where he passed Robert on his way back in.

"It's him for sure. It's 'Bandit,'" Joanna said to Piotr, her voice thick with emotion. "I don't recognize the last one. But I know who this is—Senator G... I've never seen him, or I don't remember him." She pointed to the figure standing next to the Senator, whom Byczek had called Pikuś.

All five of them moved to a round table in the adjoining room. "It's more comfortable in here," Joanna said, ushering them into her private office.

Aga caught Joanna's arm. "May I have a word with you for a moment?" she asked quietly.

They stepped over to the bar, where Aga whispered, "Robert doesn't know anything. I never told him your secret."

"Thank you," Joanna replied. "But I will need to brief him on some aspects of the case. I'm also assigning Henryk to help Aśka. We have a problem; I'll explain in a moment."

They returned to the table.

"Since Robert isn't privy to the details," Joanna began, "I'd like to explain a few things. Please, sit." She then turned to Henryk. "Do you recognize anyone from these photos?"

"Yes," he answered, pointing to Zdzira. "I only remember this girl." It was understandable; every student who partied at the Quiet Cellar knew her. The other faces, however, meant nothing to him.

"Listen," Joanna addressed both IT specialists. "Aśka and Piotr are from a business intelligence agency working on a case for me. They've discovered I'm being followed by some of the people in these photos, and that there are former Military Intelligence agents within our company leaking secrets to Senator G... These individuals are all connected in some way. From now on, you will report directly to Aśka. As IT specialists, you will assist her on this case. She will fill you in on the details." She softened her tone slightly. "And please don't be offended, but I need you to leave us now. We have other private matters to discuss."

Henryk stood. "I understand, of course. I'll await your instructions, Ms. Aśka," he said, and left. Robert, after a moment's hesitation, followed him.

"It's Pikuś, for sure," Aga said as the door closed. "He's the one Joanna confided in years ago. He, along with Zdzira and two others, started coming to parties at the club after you and Joanna disappeared. You wouldn't have known them; you were no longer in town."

Joanna sat pale and silent. Aga's words had unlocked a flood of memories. *Why hadn't she made the connection before?* The photos alone hadn't been enough. It was the combination of the images and Byczek's identification—*Pikuś*—that triggered the recall.

She had never told anyone about the second rapist. *You can't get pregnant from that,* had been her twisted rationale for the silence.

The nickname "Pikuś," spoken by Byczek and Aga, unblocked the horrifying snippets of dialogue from that night:

"Not the same hole."

Then, a nonchalant male voice from behind her:

"Me? It's a piece of cake."

This was no coincidence. Those short, brutal sentences and that nickname—"Pikuś."

"I recognize the other one, too, even though I've never seen him," she said, her voice shaking with anger. She stood up and began to pace, wringing her hands.

Piotr could see she was in a terrible state, though he didn't yet understand why. No one in the room did.

He walked to the bar, poured a glass of water, and handed it to her. "Here, please. Have a drink."

"Damn it!" she seethed, ignoring the glass. "I could have caught them earlier."

"Speak more clearly," Aga urged.

"I only heard the other one in the van. He said one sentence: 'I don't care where.'" She offered no further context.

"That's probably where the nickname comes from," Aśka observed grimly.

Piotr had never seen Joanna like this. The two deep wrinkles on her forehead and her narrowed eyes transformed her expression into one of cold, terrifying determination.

Joanna was furious—at them, but mostly at herself. Simultaneously, she felt a wave of relief. She could finally close this chapter. She knew exactly what to do. No court would ever deliver real justice to these bastards, but *her* justice would be thorough and absolute.

Piotr, however, wasn't ready to let her take the lead. "Aga, tell me everything you know about them," he said, tapping the photographs. "I didn't know them."

"I don't remember much," Aga admitted. "I just recall that after you and Joanna disappeared, these two and another guy started showing up at the club with Zdzira for a while."

Piotr began connecting the facts. He was afraid Joanna was reaching the same devastating conclusion he was. It was only a matter of time. Right now, her rage was focused on the effects, not the cause.

He walked over to Joanna, who was standing with both hands pressed against the windowpane, staring into the distance. He knew she was thinking intensely. Ignoring the others, he put his hands around her waist and pulled her close.

"I'm with you," he said. "I'll take care of this."

"No," she replied in a hard, flat voice. "You've done your part. Now it's my turn."

"You're not going to kill them, I hope," he tried to joke, lightening the mood.

"I'm not," she said. Her voice was dangerously calm. "But whether others might... I can't vouch for that."

And Joanna was to be feared. She was ruthless, relentless, cunning, and tough. So far, she had only applied those qualities in business, but Piotr thought with a pang of concern that they could be quickly transferred to other areas.

She began acting immediately, summoning her secretary and personal assistant back into the room.

"I am issuing an order," she said, her tone leaving no room for argument. "To everyone, without exception—the Presidents of the company and all my subsidiaries—they are to be here for a meeting the day after tomorrow at eight in the morning." Her gaze swept over Piotr and Aśka. "That includes you."

Piotr didn't ask why; he simply nodded.

"We'll be there, of course," Aśka said. As a division president, Aga was also included in the summons.

"Aga, honey," Joanna continued, her tone softening only slightly for her cousin, "bring all the photos you have at home tomorrow. Gather any you can get from friends and family, from any parties where they might appear."

She turned to Aśka. "Find everyone who might have known them back then. Friends, colleagues, neighbors. I don't need to explain; you're the best at what you do," she praised her.

Then, she addressed her assistant, her voice turning to steel. "I want all materials, every publication from the press, TV, or any other source with information about Mr. G... on my desk tomorrow morning. Do not overlook a single thing," she warned. "I want every detail about any shares Senator G... holds in our company or its subsidiaries, and a full report on any joint ventures we are, or have ever been, involved in."

She wasn't finished. "And at nine o'clock sharp, I want every HR manager from our company, and from every firm where we hold a majority stake or a board seat, connected remotely and ready for a briefing. No exceptions." She paused, letting the order sink in. "They are to be prepared for full, remote access to all employee files—including each other's. Also, prepare confidentiality agreements for everyone attending the meeting tomorrow. They are to be signed before anyone sets foot in the conference room. Anyone who refuses is to be escorted out immediately, their access to company data and all premises revoked on my authority. Understood?"

"Yes, Madam President," they replied, visibly intimidated.

Piotr and the others were silent. They had never seen this side of Joanna. But they knew she was absolutely right. Their opponent was a cunning and ruthless gangster who, if cornered, was capable of anything. Joanna's personal quest had just escalated into a dangerous corporate war—a conflict they would have to fight with every legal, yet utterly ruthless, means at their disposal.

Piotr's mind raced. They had already discovered that former intelligence agents, "plugs" as Aśka called them, had been planted within Joanna's corporation to sabotage it from within for a takeover. *They couldn't be allowed to succeed. This was a ticking time bomb that had to be defused,* he thought, mentally preparing for the battle ahead.

"My dears, thank you all. I have more work to do. We'll meet again tomorrow," Joanna said, dismissing the group.

Everyone began to leave, and Joanna sat down at her desk, deep in thought.

"Piotr, stay," she asked as he rose to leave. The receptionist escorted the others to the elevator.

He sat on the sofa, watching as she eventually got up and went to the bar, his mind churning over everything that had been said.

She poured herself a glass of wine. "Will you have a drink? What can I get you?"

"Yes, please. A whiskey with cola and ice."

Handing him the glass, she sat down beside him. Now calm and relaxed, she turned to him. "I know what you're thinking. You're wrong. It's not your fault. The thought would never cross my mind."

"But it crosses mine," he admitted.

"You are not the cause. *She* is. 'The Slut.' Actually, it's me. I provoked her. I called her a whore and a slut at my last party in the Quiet Cellar. She probably wanted revenge and sent them after me."

"I don't understand? And what about Pikuś?" he asked.

She was silent for a moment, wrestling with how much to reveal. No, I can't tell him everything. It won't change anything, and it might change how he feels about me.

"I don't remember everything that happened in the van," she said, choosing her words carefully. "I was just trying to survive, to breathe. They shoved the rag from the bag so deep into my throat I could barely get air. I remember one of them said to someone, 'I don't care where.' There must have been three of them. It was probably the driver, but I can't be sure." She looked away. "They were mostly silent, as if they were afraid I'd recognize a voice. That would mean they knew me before... or that I knew at least one of them."

She took a sip of wine. "It was only when Byczek said the name 'Pikuś' that the memory of that sentence came back to me," she lied, avoiding his gaze. "But maybe it's just a coincidence," she added, downing the rest of her wine in one go.

That contradicts her earlier certainty about it not being a coincidence, he thought, watching her.

He put his arm around her and held her close. "Let's just take a break from all this now," he whispered tenderly.

He was startled when she suddenly stood up. *Did I say something wrong?*

"Let's go," she said, pulling him by the hand.

Piotr, thinking she had misunderstood his intention, followed her nonetheless.

They walked to the opposite wall. Joanna pressed a hidden mechanism on a chest of drawers, and a section of the wall slid silently open, revealing a spacious living room.

"This is my private apartment," she said with an inviting gesture.

The room was large yet cozy, furnished in a modern Italian style with light, elegant furniture, armchairs, and a huge bookcase filled with books covering the far wall. The opposite side was not a wall at all, but a vast glass partition offering a breathtaking view of the Gdańsk Bay. In the distance, the multicolored sails of small yachts danced on the water, tossed by the wind. A fast passenger ferry cut across the bay on its route between Gdynia and Hel.

In the center of the room was a large, semi-elliptical sofa with a low, integrated table at its center, just the right height to comfortably reach anything placed on it.

"When do you find time to read?" he asked, gazing at the vast collection of books.

"Contrary to what you might think, I make the time. It's how I combat loneliness," she confided, the admission slipping out more honestly than she had intended. "Come on, let's go out to the terrace. The weather is beautiful."

When she opened the glass door, a warm, salty sea breeze washed over them. They stepped onto a large mezzanine furnished with summery wicker furniture. Three large, adjustable umbrellas cast a saving shade over the loungers placed by the railing. She settled onto one in a semi-reclining position, closed her eyes, and fell silent.

"I should probably be going," he said after a moment.

"Stay. Please." Her eyes remained closed. "Don't go. I'm glad you're here. Did you know you're the first person I've invited here in three years? I never bring anyone to my private space. Just rest here with me," she said, gesturing to the lounger beside her.

"Why me?" he asked, sitting down to face her.

"Because I feel... no, I *know*," she corrected herself, "that what I felt for you twenty years ago never truly went away. The memories came back, and with them, the feelings. They were always there, just buried." She still didn't open her eyes, as if afraid to see his reaction.

"I..." he began.

She took his hand and placed it over her heart. "Quiet. Let me finish," she whispered, her voice caressing and gentle, not wanting to offend him. "This isn't easy for me to say. Sometimes I feel like I'm not a woman meant to be loved. Other times, I'm ready to lose myself in love completely. But until now, I've never met anyone who measured up to you. I compared every man to you, to what I felt back then. No one was worth my love. I tried to forget you, to forget everything I felt, but I never succeeded. Now I see that was a mistake. I could have looked for you sooner. But what's done is done... and now you're here with me again." She pressed his hand against her cheek and fell silent, her eyes still shut.

"I don't know if I can give you what you're looking for," he said, "but I'm not indifferent to you. Far from it."

"I've been thinking a lot about my feelings for you," she replied. "I wasn't sure if it was just fascination, or the seed of something real. Now I know. I love you. That feeling was born in me all those years ago, and it never died. It just fell asleep, and now it has woken up. It won't be an easy love, but we'll make it work. I believe we will."

She finally opened her eyes, looking at him almost in disbelief, and then pulled him toward her.

Their kiss began carefully, gently, as if rediscovering a forgotten language. But within moments, that caution gave way to a greedy, desperate hunger. He began to undress her.

"Not here," she whispered, breaking away from his lips.

They both stood up, and without letting go of his hand, she led him back through the living room, past a door hidden in the bookcase that presumably led to a bedroom, and instead to a second door. Behind it was a bathroom dominated by a huge bathtub sunken into the floor. They entered, shedding their clothes along the way.

The next day, Piotr, Aśka, and Joanna met to review their progress. Sifting through the pile of photos Aga had collected, they realized they hadn't gained much new ground. They managed to isolate only two photos that accidentally captured persons of interest, but without dates, they were of limited use.

"This didn't help us much," Joanna remarked, frustration evident in her voice.

"Yes, but what we *do* have allows us to draw some conclusions," Aśka interjected.

"I'm listening," Joanna said.

"We should consider that the sender of the packages might not be one of the perpetrators," Aśka proposed, carefully formulating her theory. "Why would they reveal themselves like this?"

"I disagree," Piotr countered, raising his eyebrows. "It had to be one of them. Someone who was there, or who heard the story directly from the perpetrators. Otherwise, how would they know the significance of the coral beads?"

"The beads are the puzzling part," Aśka conceded, "but you might be right. They could have come into possession of them without being the actual rapist."

"Then who could it be?" Joanna asked.

"Zdzira," Aśka stated bluntly, exchanging a meaningful look with Piotr.

"What would her motive be?" Piotr asked, picking up the photo of her.

"There could be two motives," Aśka said, standing up and beginning to pace. "One is blackmail. She's softening you up with these deliveries before making a demand. The second is revenge. That seems more likely to me. Revenge on her old 'buddies.'"

"After so many years?" Joanna's tone was skeptical.

"She probably believes you have the resources to exact a more effective revenge than she does, and she's not wrong. However, she's not particularly cunning. She made a serious mistake in thinking you wouldn't be able to trace it back to her."

"That would fit," Joanna mused. "But if that's the case, we should expect more packages. There were more beads on the original necklace."

"The crucial question," Aśka added, "is how she came to possess those specific corals in the first place."

A cold wave of realization washed over Joanna. Of course. She had been wearing that necklace at the Quiet Cellar on the night she had quarreled with Zdzira. She could still hear the woman's mocking voice: *"Only peasants wear beads like that."*

"There are still the photos themselves," Joanna said, turning back to Aśka. "We need to find the photographer who took them. Maybe that will give us another piece of the puzzle."

"If he wasn't an accredited press photographer, it won't be easy to find him. But I'll take care of it," Aśka declared.

"Two of these photos definitely show the perpetrators, and I will deal with them personally," Joanna stated, her voice firm. "I'm not yet completely convinced that our theory about Zdzira setting me up is correct, so please focus your efforts on verifying that thoroughly."

"And how is the search for my daughters going?" she asked, turning her head toward Piotr and changing the subject.

She must think this topic is less painful, or perhaps it's just too difficult for her to dwell on the rape any longer, he thought. He responded quickly.

"We've hit a wall at the hospital where you gave birth. The documents make no mention of twins. We're now checking all the adoption centers and tracking down the staff who worked there at the time. Unfortunately, most are deceased, and those who are alive don't remember much. Aśka has access to all the archives from that period, but the adoption procedures back then listed the mother as 'NN'—Unknown. The children were given the surnames of their new parents, who also chose their first names. The only comforting news is that all the documents exist and haven't been destroyed. We do have some leads, but it's too early to draw any conclusions. I can tell you that they point toward your solicitor in London. He discovered something and then covered his tracks. We don't yet know why he didn't inform you or why he hid the documents he obtained from the hospital. I'll get to the bottom of it. I'm sure a trip to London will be necessary soon."

Joanna nodded, then leaned forward as if to share a secret, her voice dropping to a determined whisper.

"Legally, I can't prove anything to make the justice system hold them accountable. But I can use my company to hit them where it hurts most. For men like them, the worst thing is to be stripped of everything they have. I'm going to buy their shares, take over their companies, and create competing enterprises to drive them out of business. We will discover their illegal dealings, expose them publicly, and let the relevant state authorities handle the fallout. That will be your task, Aśka." Joanna's voice was strong and unwavering. "I will bankrupt them all," she added, rising from her desk.

"You'll face fierce resistance from them and everyone involved. It could be dangerous," Piotr noted, his tone full of concern.

Just then, Aśka's phone vibrated insistently.

"Answer it," Joanna said.

"I'm sorry, it's urgent. Yes, I'm listening," Aśka said, her face suddenly clouding. A long moment of silence followed. "Yes, I understand. Notify the police. Keep me updated."

"What happened?" Piotr asked.

"They lost The Dog, but they found traces of blood."

"Explain."

"The two agents tailing him saw him enter an alley and disappear. They stayed with his car. After a few minutes, another man got in and drove off. One agent went to check the alley while the other followed the car. Janek just reported fresh bloodstains in a corner of the yard leading down to a basement. That's all for now. They'll report back if they find anything more. But I don't like the look of that blood," she concluded.

"Going back to our plan," Piotr began, "you have to be strategic. Move in secret, and only strike when you hold all the cards. I will concentrate on finding your daughters, and Aśka will focus on Senator G... and Bandit."

"Tomorrow, we begin screening all my key employees," Joanna stated. "Of course, word will get out. So, Aśka, you and Henryk need to be ready to monitor all communications. I want to catch anyone who makes contact with Senator G... or with any of the former intelligence assets we're about to root out."

"We're ready. We'll catch them all," Aśka said firmly.

From the very next morning, the DLACOM office building was buzzing like a disturbed beehive.

"What's going on?" was the most frequently asked question in that part of Gdynia.

No one knew anything concrete, only that they were required to read and sign a stringent loyalty document.

The process began in the conference room, where individuals entered one by one, surprised to see the head of DLACOM presiding alongside several unfamiliar faces. The first to be summoned were the HR officers from various company branches. Only afterward were specific managers and executives called in.

The head of HR began by reviewing her own staff, then assisted Aśka and Henryk in investigating individuals they flagged. Together, they worked to uncover the hidden periods of service their targets had spent in the Military Intelligence (WSI). No one listed this on their CV; they had failed vetting and hidden this chapter of their careers with fabricated stories about working for fictitious companies. These were often defunct state-owned enterprises, bankrupt shell companies, or fictional foreign internships in distant, exotic countries.

One of the first significant catches was a Vice-President who had liaised with a major state-owned enterprise. Aśka uncovered an eight-year gap in his history, supposedly spent at 'Szczecin Polservis,' from where he was allegedly delegated to a post in Congo. His references were forged, and the company itself never existed.

The outcome was always the same. The individual was asked to step into an adjoining room. There, the Chief Human Resources Officer, flanked by three of her staff, two lawyers, and two security guards, was waiting. They meticulously reviewed the person's employment contract, then presented them with immediate dismissal or contract termination papers. They were ordered to surrender all company property—phones, car keys, documents, and access passes. Security then escorted them out through a side exit, and they were instantly locked out of the company's systems and premises. A notification was immediately sent to their department about the access ban.

By evening, eighteen people had been dismissed from DLACOM. The scale of the infiltration was a shock to Joanna; she hadn't anticipated such deep compromise within her company. When she realized that one of her fairly close colleagues was among them, she got up from the table and followed him out.

"Why?" she asked.

"I'm sorry, Joasia. I never harmed you or the company, but I had no choice. Once you're in, there's no way out. They never let you go," he replied, hanging his head as he walked toward the exit.

"Come see me the day after tomorrow," she said to his retreating back, turning on her heel. It wasn't out of regret, but from a sudden intuition that he might still be useful to her.

The next morning, the front pages of all the newspapers were dominated by the "purge at DLACOM." Yet, no one knew what had truly happened. The media speculated about a corporate reorganization and a desire to rejuvenate the senior management. Notably, no journalist managed to secure an interview with Joanna—except for Aśka. This, however, was a deliberate and calculated move.

"You have to feed a narrative to the media," Aśka had argued. "Otherwise, they'll invent their own and start writing nonsense."

None of the fired employees disclosed the real reasons for their dismissal. This was understandable; admitting to being a former intelligence plant would permanently blacklist them from any significant future employment.

Joanna's next move was financial warfare. She established two shell companies in tax havens—one in the Cayman Islands, the other in the Bahamas. Their sole purpose was to quietly acquire shares in Senator G...'s publicly traded companies. At first, the Senator was pleased to see his stock prices rising. By the time he realized a hostile takeover was underway, it was too late. He had lost control.

Simultaneously, Joanna created a separate corporate entity to target "Bandit's" sprawling business empire. "This will take more time," she explained to her team. "We can't crush his operations overnight, especially since his companies are privately held, scattered across Poland, and operate in various industries. I'm giving myself a year." From that moment, she began to execute her plan with meticulous precision.

It took Senator G... nearly three weeks to grasp that something was fundamentally wrong. On the surface, nothing had changed, but the ownership of his companies was steadily shifting into the hands of two mysterious corporate entities. It was a devastating blow, and the takeover accelerated. Over the next month, these offshore companies bought out almost all the minority shareholders, offering prices so inflated that no one could refuse.

Once the shell companies held a majority stake, they installed their own management, who promptly liquidated the companies' valuable assets. These assets were then sold off to the companies' former employees at absurdly low prices. The move made no economic sense, but it achieved its true goal: it stripped Senator G... of his property and wealth.

Joanna was careful to never let the targeted companies go into bankruptcy or formal liquidation, avoiding the appointment of a court-mandated trustee. "A trustee is the last resort," Piotr had warned her. "You never know who they really work for. It's worse than the mafia because it's all seemingly legal. Where this much money is involved, the law becomes powerless. Significant assets never fall into random hands; they always go to someone from the 'right' arrangement."

While Joanna was cleansing her corporation, Pikuś was conducting a purge of his own, albeit with cruder methods. With his dim-witted but fiercely obedient enforcer in tow, he walked down a grimy street near the Main Railway Station, heading for a small beer hall by the Market Hall. He was there to find Byczek. He walked with the grim determination of a man tasked with cleaning up a mess. The Bandit's words echoed in his head: *"You need to sort this out. I don't believe Byczek went to Zdzira's for no reason. He's piecing something together, and he's a threat. So for your own sake, make sure you don't end up like everyone else who thought this world runs on coincidences."*

The pungent smell from a fetid latrine behind a nearby fence signaled his arrival. The beer hall, its sign faded with age, greeted them with a mocking sign on the door: "We don't serve alcohol to intoxicated persons"—a stark contradiction to the scene inside. Pikuś never frequented such dives; he hadn't needed to since Zdzira began presiding over her own sanctuary of vice.

He spotted Byczek immediately. The man was slumped in a corner, hunched over an unfinished beer mug. His once powerful frame was still imposing, though the years had carved deep furrows into his face, making him look like a ploughed field.

They approached. Byczek glanced up, held their gaze for a moment, then slowly turned back to his beer.

What's this? Pikuś thought. He doesn't recognize us?

"Byczek, what the fuck? You don't recognize your old buddies anymore?" he snarled.

Byczek turned his head slowly, then reached into his pocket. Pikuś watched the movement nervously, a flash of panic wondering if he was going for a weapon. He relaxed only when he saw a glasses case.

"Guess the old man can't see too well," Pikuś muttered to his soldier.

"You don't know shit about what I see," Byczek grumbled, putting on the glasses—a recent purchase since he'd started a night watchman job.

Pikuś pulled up a chair. "Looks like you've been making new friends," he growled.

"I've got a business proposition. You could earn a lot," Pikuś said, his tone shifting to a false, reassuring calm.

"Talk, then get lost. I want to be alone."

A heavyset waitress with sagging breasts ambled over. "Two beers," Pikuś ordered quickly. She then glared at the enforcer standing behind him. "You gonna loiter all day? Order something or get out."

The thug, bewildered, shouted over the din, "A beer for me! A pint!" unaware that pints were the only size served.

"You visited our mutual friend on some half-baked business," Pikuś began, his voice deceptively casual.

"So what? A man's allowed, right?" Byczek retorted.

"We're interested in where you've been and who you've been talking to."

"You're too small-time to play in that league. But this information could cost your friends a fortune. They have money. Me, I'm just a friendly guy."

"Twenty," he added.

"Twenty what?"

"Thousands. In U.S. dollars."

"Fifteen," Pikuś shot back angrily, thinking of the Bandit's budget. The sheer amount Byczek was asking was proof in itself that the head of DLACOM was involved.

"Bring the cash tomorrow, and we'll talk details," Pikuś tried again.

"Don't get smart. Just get lost. Conversation's over," Byczek said, straightening up to his full height. "Come back here tomorrow with the money, and you'll find out everything."

"Let's go," Pikuś said to his companion. He stood up slowly, pushing his chair back. "I'll be here tomorrow at the same time," he told Byczek, then turned and headed for the exit.

Once they were outside, Pikuś turned to the man trailing behind him. Through clenched teeth, he articulated slowly, "Ed, he's yours. You know what to do."

"When?"

"Tonight. Make it a clean job. No complications—you get the idea."

"Sure. No trouble," Ed replied, pleased at the prospect of the large sum he would earn for such a task. It was standard for these kinds of orders.

"I'm going to clean up at Zdzira's," Pikuś told him, then headed for the taxi rank.

Ed lurked among the nearby outdoor market stalls. He shifted his weight nervously from foot to foot, smoking one cigarette after another while keeping his eyes fixed on the beer hall's door. When Byczek's silhouette finally appeared in the doorway, he stubbed his cigarette out under a dirty shoe.

He had no concrete plan, as Pikuś hadn't given him one. He figured he would just follow Byczek and take care of him at the first good opportunity—as long as it didn't turn out like that mess with the journalist, he thought, furious with himself for that botched job.

Meanwhile, unsuspecting, Byczek walked along the sidewalk toward the parking lot where he was due to start his guard duty in half an hour. His job was to protect a large area containing two barracks and parking for a dozen or so official and private cars. He was walking alongside the perimeter fence, nearing the entrance gate, when a man in a pulled-down cap blocked his path. The man's head was bowed as if he were searching for something on the pavement.

Byczek was about to step around him when an alarm bell went off in his head—*It's one of Pikuś's bastards!* But the realization came a fraction of a second too late. The flash of a long blade was already arcing toward his heart. He managed only a slight twist to the left. The knife sank into his body just below the collarbone.

The sharp, searing pain triggered a primal reaction. He fell back on the instincts of his youth, when he'd responded to violence with even greater violence. He took two quick steps back. The attacker, unsure if his blow had been fatal, hesitated, forfeiting his chance for a second strike. He stood waiting for Byczek to collapse.

But Byczek didn't fall. He stood his ground for a second, then yanked off his jacket and wrapped it around his right forearm. In a flash, he lunged at Ed. The attacker swung the knife again, but Byczek took the blow on his padded arm. The force staggered Ed, and in that moment, Byczek seized his other arm by the wrist and neck, locking him in an iron grip. Ed thrashed violently, and they both crashed against the fence.

Out of the corner of his eye, Byczek saw a loose strand of barbed wire dangling from above. He grabbed it with his free hand and, in one brutal motion, looped it twice around his attacker's neck, yanked it tight, and jumped back. He held the sharp, twisted end in his bare hand, and blood now dripped freely from his palm, spattering the ground.

The attacker hung limply against the fence, the knife clattering from his open hand. A terrible, whistling gurgle escaped his throat as he fought for air. His hands flew up, fingers desperately trying to pry the barbed wire from his neck. His eyes began to glaze over, his breath catching in ragged bursts, until finally, his hands fell limp at his sides.

Seeing this, Byczek stepped forward, grabbed him by the chin, and loosened the deadly pressure. He unwound the wire, threaded the end back through the fence mesh, and twisted it into a secure tangle. The man's eyes followed him, and to Byczek's surprise, he saw a flicker of gratitude in them for sparing his life.

"Damn, I got off easy. I'm too old for this shit," he muttered. With his bloody hand, he grabbed his phone and hit the speed dial.

"What's up? You running late or something?" his colleague from the parking lot answered.

"I'm about two hundred meters out, near checkpoint three."

"I've been attacked. Call the police and get over here. I'm securing the scene," he added, a note of grim pride in his voice.

As he moved past a military transport vehicle parked nearby, a flash of light from the headquarters building, about three hundred meters away, caught his eye. *A window opening?* he thought, surprised. *They have air conditioning in there.*

Instinctively, he raised a hand to his glasses, squinting for a better look. The moment he turned his head, a burning impact slammed into the left side of his face, right next to his ear. The simultaneous *spang* of a bullet ricocheting off the transporter's armor plate made the reality clear: he was being shot at.

He hit the ground and, rolling across the sun-baked sand, scrambled under the vehicle for cover. He braced for the "corrected" second, more accurate shot. Peering cautiously from his low position, he saw that the roofline of a nearby building now completely blocked the sniper's line of fire. *He's not a professional,* Byczek thought. *A pro wouldn't have missed from that distance.*

He touched the burning spot on his head. His hand came away covered in blood. His left ear was grazed; he had been a centimeter from death. That slight turn of his head had saved him. After waiting a moment longer, he crawled out from his hiding place.

Two soldiers walking past glanced at him with surprise, took in his bloodied state, then averted their eyes and continued on. *They don't want any trouble with us here,* he reflected.

He carefully examined the side of the transporter where the bullet had struck, noting a fresh scratch and a bright mark. Crouching low to stay out of the sniper's sightline, he ran his hand over the sand where the ricochet would have landed. After a moment, his fingers found a warm spot. He dug in and pulled out a flattened piece of the bullet.

Staying in a crouch, he moved toward the barracks, only straightening up when he was a meter from the wall. He wiped his sweaty, blood-smeared forehead. He felt no pain, but a single thought pounded in his head: *What have I stumbled onto that they want me dead? Are they trying to stop me from returning to Poland? What do I know that I don't even realize I know?*

He mentally scanned the huge pile of documents, reports, and business notes he'd read over the past few days.

Nothing. A complete blank.

Once inside the barracks, he pressed the emergency button on his phone, alerting security that he was in mortal danger. He went to the TV room where several soldiers were watching a recorded football match and sat in a corner with his back to the wall, the main entrance in full view. He drew his pistol, laid it on his lap, and waited, his hand clenched around the grip.

About five minutes later, two guards from the GROM unit entered. One flashed his ID, approached, and whispered the code phrase: "CBA – Condor."

They flanked him and hurried him to a Humvee idling outside. The driver sped off toward the gate.

"We're going to the safe house," one of the guards said.

Kowalczyk (Byczek) wasn't fooled by their Military Police uniforms; he knew at least one was a CBA agent.

"What happened?" the agent asked, nodding at his bloody ear.

"Sniper," he replied, and gave a quick account of the attack. One of the guards was on the phone the entire time, receiving orders that redirected them to an American logistics base. Kowalczyk was to wait there for the next flight back to Poland. An escort vehicle cleared their path, its horn scattering the sparse traffic.

I'm burned, he realized. I know something so dangerous they've decided to kill me. It's time to go home.

After passing through security at the gate, they entered a mission building used by American logistics troops cooperating with Polish military intelligence under NATO. A few rooms were occupied by a front—a "Polish trading company" that was, in fact, a covert station for translators and two military counterintelligence agents overseeing the investigation. From here, orders were sent in a way that bypassed even the highest command at the Ghazni base.

He was given a separate room in the hotel section, and the blue pass he received restricted him to that area only. He wasn't particularly worried. His mission in Afghanistan was over. *I can wrap this up from Poland,* he thought as he walked to his room. *If I survive.*

He lay down on the bed, still in his clothes, and fell asleep almost instantly. His rest was short. Around midnight, he got up and walked to the window. Incredibly, a dream had provided the missing link—it made him understand *why* he was a target. It was a connection he might never have made consciously, and the assassination attempt had indirectly led him to the truth. The implication was so staggering and dangerous that he couldn't sleep for the rest of the night.

I can't trust anyone. Not my closest colleagues, and certainly not my superiors—especially General Z... and his people.

I have to get what I know to someone else, just in case, he concluded. He decided to do something insane and utterly unforgivable in the world of intelligence.

He took his laptop, connected to the internet, and composed an encrypted message. The recipient was Piotr's investigative firm—or, to be more precise, Aśka.

Aśka stared at the encrypted email that had just appeared on her screen.

"What in the hell is this?" she wondered. This address was known only to a handful of her trusted IT contacts. She knew their aliases from years of collaborating to breach the security of various corporations and institutions. She didn't know all these hackers personally—some operated under strange pseudonyms and prized their anonymity. The sender's handle was unfamiliar; she had never corresponded with him before.

Has someone betrayed me? was her first thought, but she quickly dismissed it as paranoia. She immediately traced the message's origin and checked the sender's IP and nickname.

"It's an emergency," she understood the moment she saw the location: Afghanistan.

She easily decrypted the data using her custom decryption program. The cipher wasn't particularly complex, almost as if it had been tailored for her capabilities. This infuriated her; it meant the sender had cracked one of her old passwords and had access to her work computer. *How is that possible?* She ran through all the possibilities. *Is it one of my hacker friends? He deliberately used a new alias—what is he so afraid of?*

The content of the message stunned her to her core. *The sender is in mortal danger, and he's using me as his dead man's switch,* she realized after reading just the first few paragraphs. Her astonishment only grew as she read on.

She grabbed her phone and sent a text to Piotr: **Coming to you now. Urgent.**

"I'll be right back," she said to Henryk, her new boyfriend. She threw on some clothes and hurried out. For the past few weeks, she had been living with Henryk, the IT specialist from Joanna's company. Their shared passions had blossomed into a relationship, and they were testing the waters by living together.

Piotr was in Joanna's apartment, his long, delicate fingers massaging her bare back, when his phone blared its alarm from the nightstand. Startled, he looked up. Aśka only used that signal for matters of critical importance.

"I'm sorry, Joasia, this is important!"

He read her second message: **Check your mail – URGENT.**

"I'll be right back," he said, his tone that of a disappointed masseur, and kissed her shoulder before leaving.

He went to the office Joanna had set up for him in a quiet part of the house, turned on the computer, and read with growing curiosity.

...I am an agent. My mission was to investigate your company's interest in the activities of Senator G... and his associate "Bandit," specifically their cooperation with the military regarding the overhaul of combat equipment in Afghanistan. I believe the individuals listed below form an organized criminal group that has monopolized the military procurement market. Repairs in Poland were conducted only on paper, with falsified reports. Non-functional equipment was sent back to Afghanistan, only to return to Senator G...'s facilities for another round of "repairs." These fictitious repairs have cost the state budget millions of zlotys, distributed among all participants in this scheme. Two hours ago, an unidentified sniper tried to kill me. My findings implicate high-ranking military officials, including one of my direct superiors. This prevents me from reporting my discoveries through official channels.

Your journalistic duty is to protect your sources. From now on, I am one of them, and I am placing my life in your hands. At the next meeting of General Z...'s Military Staff, there will be an attempt to physically eliminate individuals directly involved in Senator G...'s corrupt activities. My contact is Karolina, Senator G...'s assistant. Use the password: CLEANER.

Involved in this scandal are: General Z..., Colonel Ludwisiak, and Captain Dębski. They form the core of this operation. There are others, the most dangerous being Major Zenon K....

I do not know how the commander of the Task Force in Afghanistan plans to eliminate direct witnesses.

In past civilian matters, I have cooperated with you under the alias "Lark" - YPL 28176453 92826g7183ahju HTA—hence this message being sent to you.

Attached is a compressed, encrypted file containing all details—to be opened only in the event of my death.

Piotr was still processing this when he turned and found Aśka already standing over him.

"What do you make of it?" she asked.

"High-stakes, but the credibility is zero," he said, getting up and pacing nervously. "Aśka, prepare an article for your paper for tomorrow. We need to go public with some of these details—it might be the only way to protect our informant. The meeting he mentions is in Warsaw the day after tomorrow; I've confirmed it. Move quickly. At the editorial office, share the details only with the Editor-in-Chief. And take two of our security guys with you—consider all materials you're carrying to be under active protection."

The next morning, just before ten, Aśka was sipping hot coffee from a paper cup, reviewing the article one last time before facing the Editor-in-Chief. The clatter of her keyboard had been her soundtrack since 5 a.m. as she scoured the military bulletins of the Ministry of Defense. The steel eagle logo seemed to mock her. The betrayal of high-ranking officers, their oath broken, was a profoundly depressing spectacle.

She walked decisively into his office.

"Hello. What have you got for me?" he asked.

"Something for the front page. Read it." She handed him the printout.

He gestured for her to sit. The silence as he read lasted just long enough for her to start doubting her decision. The magazine hadn't had a major scoop in some time. The boss, leaning back in his chair, his striped shirt straining at his belly, nodded slowly as he read.

"Bomb!" he finally said. The word guaranteed publication. The Chief was a staunch defender of free speech, his views a mix of defending democratic principles and a zeal for exposing government corruption.

"Evidence. I need hard evidence. Do you have it?"

"I do."

"Such as?"

"The testimony of a CBA agent—his operational findings. The attempt on his life at the Ghazni base confirms his claims. His information aligns with the intelligence my own firm has gathered. We have the drug smuggling discovery at the container terminal, the connections between Senator G... and top military officials. It's his company that handles the equipment refurbishment from Afghanistan."

She threw a stack of photographs onto his desk.

"Yes, yes. This is something," he barked, flipping through them.

"The District Prosecutor's Office in Poznań has confirmed an investigation is underway," she added, handing him supporting documents. "We have plenty of other leads."

"For now, we'll publish our version of events without names or photos. Adjust the text accordingly," he commanded.

"Is that all?" she snapped, angry at the dilution.

"We must maintain objectivity. That's fundamental. Reliability above all. You have no live witnesses to confirm this, and publishing this will cause an earthquake across the military and beyond. You're accusing the highest military authorities in Poland of corruption, attempted murder, drug smuggling, embezzlement, and running a criminal group. Is that not enough for you? And your proof is an email from an unknown source, a few photos, a prosecutor's confirmation of an investigation, and some unverifiable hacker intel. It's not enough."

"We can discuss my professional methods another time. For now, evaluate the evidence and decide. Or would you prefer signed affidavits from the thugs themselves?" she shot back. She couldn't reveal her sources.

"I'm the one sticking my neck out here!" he said, irritated. "Get me witnesses, and we'll publish the names."

"Fine. You'll have them in a few days. But I want this story to run *now*, exactly as I've written it."

She turned and slammed the door, missing the contented smile that spread across his face. He hadn't expected her to cave so easily.

She still had a lot to do. Walking down the corridor toward the exit, she ignored the stares and soft whispers that followed her. Without turning, she raised a finger in a triumphant gesture.

She ran down the stairs, unable to hide her joy. This was a real bombshell, and it was hers.

Merging with the crowd on the pavement, she didn't notice the man who had been tailing her since she left the building. He moved closer, hiding behind other pedestrians, closing the distance to just a few meters. As she turned the corner, he stopped pretending and followed her directly toward a nearby parking lot.

She passed through a wide entrance into a large square packed with cars, where her Mercedes was parked. Navigating the tight rows of vehicles that stretched from the sidewalk railings to the building opposite, she suddenly noticed a man ahead of her wearing a cap pulled low over his eyes. *Just like the ones my own operatives use,* she had time to think, before he turned sharply toward her, a knife flashing in his right hand.

He made a wide, upward swing, aiming for her stomach. She instinctively blocked with the purse she was carrying, which absorbed the worst of the impact, but the force of the blow still sent the bag—knife and all—hard into her abdomen. Reacting instantly, she used the momentum, stepping back half a pace, pivoting on her heel, and delivering a powerful roundhouse kick to his head. He crashed into a nearby car and then slumped to the ground, his eyes wide with shock.

But a second later, he was scrambling back to his feet, searching for his target. Aśka didn't wait for a second attack. She sprinted to her car, yanked the door open, slid behind the wheel, locked the doors, and sped toward the exit, her hand pressed firmly on the horn to clear a path.

Once she merged onto a busy two-lane avenue, she called Piotr.

"I was just assaulted! Someone tried to kill me!" she said, her voice tight with adrenaline.

"Where are you?"

"I'm in the car, driving to the office."

"Okay. Drive as fast as you safely can. I'll be waiting in the underground parking lot with security."

When she pulled into the secure parking garage, she was met by Piotr's team, who immediately surrounded her car. They quickly escorted her into the building, forming a protective cordon around her. A part of her was almost pleased by the show of force. Sitting at her desk with a cup of soothing fruit tea, she recounted the attack in the parking lot.

They all agreed on one crucial point: this was not a random robbery.

Aśka made it clear that her role in exposing the intelligence agents within DLACOM, combined with her investigation into Senator G... and the revelations from the mysterious CBA informant, had drawn dangerous attention. While attracting the interest of the special services was one thing, the real danger came from the individuals whose annihilation would be guaranteed by her going public. They were almost certainly behind this attack.

Piotr immediately dispatched two men to secure the footage from the parking lot's security cameras, knowing it was their best chance to identify the assailant quickly.

With their assessment aligned, they decided to leave for Warsaw immediately.

CHAPTER VI
CONFESSION

The next day, Aśka called Piotr. Her voice was sharp with anger and distress.

"Piotr, my mother was taken to the hospital by ambulance. I'm on my way there now. Don't wait for me."

"Which hospital? I'll come right away."

"On Kashubian Square," she added, and hung up.

The previous evening, when Aśka had spoken to her, her mother had complained of pain and feeling unwell.

"Mommy, I'll come over."

"No, you don't have to. I'm not alone; your father is taking care of me. He even made dinner today," she had said with a laugh.

Aśka spent half the day at the hospital, ensuring her mother was diagnosed quickly and received good care. After all the tests were done, a visit from the head doctor—a grey-haired, kind older man—sent a chill down her spine. She understood immediately that her mother was seriously ill. He informed her that her mother had suffered an embolism that could be life-threatening.

Piotr arrived quickly, just half an hour after her. He had a doctor friend who worked at that hospital and wanted to help, but no intervention was needed. Aśka had already personally ensured her mother was receiving meticulous attention. She was lying in a two-person room, connected to an IV drip and a monitor tracking her vital signs.

Not wanting to be underfoot, Piotr lingered in the corridor, occasionally popping his head in to comfort Aśka and bringing her coffee from the vending machine. His presence began to agitate her, so she finally shooed him away.

"Piotr, it's nice that you're here, but there's nothing more you can do. If I need you, I'll call."

"Are you sure?" he asked.

"Of course. Please, just go."

She sat on a chair by the bed. Her father had gone to buy some necessities and bottled water.

Her mother opened her eyes. Seeing Aśka, a smile lit up her face. With great difficulty, she began to speak. Aśka leaned in close to hear her better.

"Back then, in the hospital..." she began, her breathing quick and shallow. "I gave birth to a very sick child... a girl. She died immediately."

"When? What hospital?" Aśka asked, not understanding. *She must be delirious,* she thought.

"I didn't give birth to you," her mother whispered. "I stole you. But there was another little girl... your sister."

She paused, gathering her strength to continue. "I was alone in the maternity ward. The doctor was busy saving someone else. I was young, and strong... I wanted a child so badly. I got up... and I switched the bracelets on your wrists. Forgive me." Her head fell back onto the pillow. "Your father... he never knew," she whispered, before sinking into unconsciousness.

Aśka stood petrified, staring at her mother's pained and exhausted face. *What in God's name is she talking about?!* "Mommy! Mommy!" she burst into tears, hugging her and kissing her worn hands. She pressed the emergency button and held it down until a doctor rushed in. He checked her pulse and looked at the monitor.

"She's sleeping. It's better this way," he told Aśka.

She never regained consciousness. She died three days later.

When a sobbing Aśka told Piotr, he said without a moment's hesitation, "You have as much time off as you need. Take care of everything. Use any resources you need and get to the bottom of this."

After the funeral, she spent two weeks making arrangements. She did nothing else, and the busywork helped her survive the immediate shock of the loss. She also had to care for her father, who was completely broken. He moved in with her temporarily, and they supported each other through their grief.

Piotr provided discreet and sensitive support, helping her through it all. Their conversations became more substantive as she made progress in unraveling the mystery. However, the final revelation would be a shock to both of them—and not only to them.

Summer was in full swing, and after several weeks, Piotr and Joanna were spending more and more of their days and nights together. In the evenings, Joanna found she could barely function without Piotr nearby. *It's like a second youth, a first love,* she analyzed her own emotional involvement. *If he wanted to live with me... but it would be best to get away, somewhere far away where no one knows us.* She knew that dream was attainable, but only after they had solved the mystery of the threatening packages and neutralized the associated dangers.

Piotr was now staying overnight at her mansion more often, leaving in the morning for the office where Aśka was tirelessly working to decipher her mother's deathbed confession.

The first thing Aśka did was visit the hospital where her mother had supposedly given birth.

The elderly director of the hospital, upon seeing Aśka's press card, looked at her with undisguised reluctance. She had always associated journalists with trouble.

"How can I help you?" she asked, her tone artificially pleasant.

"I'm looking for information on a girl born here 28 years ago."

"My dear, that's not really my department. You'd need to check the archives, though I'm not sure all the files from that period have been preserved. You have my permission. I'll notify the archivist of your visit immediately."

When she went down to the hospital basement, she was greeted by a young man with a tired, sallow face. After she explained she was looking for hospital records from 28 years ago, he led her to a remote shelf stacked with gray folders covered in a thick layer of dust.

"Here is what you're looking for," he said, then walked away, leaving her alone.

After sifting through birth certificates, death certificates, employee rosters, and numerous documents for children relinquished for adoption, she had gathered enough to continue her search on the computer.

"You know, I just remembered something," the archivist said as she passed him on her way out.

"What's that?" she asked, looking at him curiously.

He took a step back, as if to leave.

"Speak. Now," she demanded.

He lowered his gaze, intimidated by her stern posture.

"But... it costs money," he managed to cough out.

"How much?" Her voice warmed with a feigned friendliness, trying not to scare him off.

"A hundred," he mumbled.

"Of course," she said, pulling out a hundred-zloty note and handing it to him.

His trembling hand greedily snatched the bill and stuffed it into his pocket. *He's a drug addict,* she thought, looking into his unnaturally dilated pupils.

"A few years ago, there was a guy here looking for the same thing you are."

"How do you know what I was looking for?"

"The director. She called me."

"When was this, and who was he?"

"About three years ago. He was a foreigner, had a strange, dull accent."

"What else?"

"Nothing."

"Did he take anything? Make copies?"

"No, nothing like that. But he was happy. He gave me a lot of money for basically nothing. I was just supposed to tell no one he was here."

"Well, it's nice you didn't keep that promise."

She left convinced she was one step away from solving the mystery. She wondered for a moment whether to call Piotr and share what she had learned.

No, better not. This is my private business, she decided, resolving to inform him the next day.

The following day, she placed her report on his desk.

"Have a look," she asked.

Piotr leaned over the report. When he finished, the surprise on his face confirmed that they would never have uncovered this without the clues from Aśka's dying mother.

They began working the new angle. They made good progress, and after a few days, they received the first significant piece of information—it was so surprising that Piotr asked Aśka for more time.

"Give me two more days," he said to her, just as she was about to reveal her own discovery.

"Why two days?"

"I still have to check one more thing."

When the long-awaited envelope arrived on his desk, he opened it eagerly and read the contents. A sigh of relief escaped his chest.

He stood up quickly, slipped the envelope into a drawer, and considered his next move as he walked to Aśka's office. He stepped in confidently, a look of triumph on his face.

"Get ready for noon today," he told her.

"I'm ready," Aśka replied with a firm nod.

"Are you sure you want this?" Piotr asked, ensuring he had her full consent. "It will change your entire life."

"Yes, of course I do. My mother wanted this too, by telling me about it," she reminded him.

Piotr called Joanna. Earlier that morning, before leaving for work, he had told her in a mysterious tone, "Keep your entire day open for me. I have a very important matter to discuss with you."

"Then tell me now."

"No, I can't right now—I still have some things to arrange. I'll just say that it's something personal, very personal. I have to go," he'd added, quickly leaving before she could press him for more details.

He called her now.

"Are you ready? Can I come over?" he asked.

"What is so important?" she asked, her curiosity piqued.

"We're going to celebrate," was all he would reveal, refusing to explain the occasion.

They arranged to meet at her apartment at noon.

She sat in an armchair, gazing thoughtfully out the window. *Is he going to propose?* she wondered. She had been waiting for it. She had long since suggested they move in together; the constant back-and-forth was exhausting. Besides, everyone knew about them since the paparazzi had photographed them kissing. The tabloids had buzzed for a while, but things had eventually quieted down.

Piotr arrived at her apartment punctually at noon, dressed formally and carrying a bottle of champagne.

"And where are the flowers?" she teased, slightly amazed. "A proposal without flowers? Probably the fashion now—but not mine," she commented silently.

He greeted her as always, with a kiss on the lips. Then he walked to the bar and placed the champagne inside. Her eyes followed him, but she couldn't read anything from his expression. She began to feel nervous. *Maybe it's not what I thought.*

He sat down opposite her, looked into her eyes with a hint of uncertainty, and then immediately glanced away.

She waited impatiently.

However, Piotr began from a completely different angle. She was so surprised that he had to repeat his question.

"What genetic material did you give that detective for comparison when you had me checked?" he asked Joanna.

"Hair from one of the locks in the envelope. Why do you ask?" The visible disappointment on her face did not escape Piotr's notice.

"I'll explain in a moment. Tell me, were there two genetic samples? And were they tested separately, or just one?"

"No, I only gave hair from one lock," she explained.

"That's exactly what I thought," he said, still avoiding her gaze.

"Piotr, tell me what's going on. I can see you're trying to hide something from me."

"Not from you, but for you."

"Piotr, for heaven's sake, speak clearly! No more riddles."

"I don't know if you're ready to hear what I have to say. Please, sit down," he added as she tried to stand up, upset by his words.

He took her hand and gently guided her back onto the sofa. He brought her a glass of water and placed it on the table beside her.

She watched him, her eyes wide with fear. The last time someone had treated her with such gravity, she had learned of her parents' death in a train crash. Now, her heart was in her throat, her breathing was fast, and she was habitually wringing her hands.

"Don't be upset. I have to tell you something, but I don't know how to start." He ran a hand through his hair and looked away again.

"You're leaving me," she whispered, for no reason she could name.

He leaned over and kissed her passionately on the lips, a long, reassuring kiss.

"I would sooner die than leave you," he assured her. "I love you."

"Then what is this about?" Relief was audible in Joanna's voice.

"It's about your children."

"Speak, please. Don't keep me in suspense any longer."

"You gave birth to twins. That's an indisputable fact. The second fact is that they were separated and raised apart."

"How do you know that?" she reacted nervously.

"More on that later. The locks of hair in the envelope belonged to two different children, but one of them is not genetically yours. It follows that we still don't know if I am the father of your children. It depends on which lock of hair you submitted for analysis."

"Piotr, what are you talking about?" she burst out. On the other hand, she knew he would never put her under such stress if he hadn't verified everything meticulously. "I'm sorry... keep talking."

"Your mother didn't know about it," he continued. "That's why she wrote what she did. No one knew. Except for the woman who switched your daughter."

"My God! Piotr, how is that possible?" She still didn't understand.

"Normally, it shouldn't have been. But this woman was in the hospital where you gave birth. She was lying next to you, separated only by a screen."

"Piotr, please... speak more clearly."

"One of your daughters has been found," he finally said, revealing what he had wanted to tell her from the beginning.

She jumped to her feet, knocking over the glass of water on the table. She rushed to him, grabbed his shoulders, and looked directly into his eyes. "Where is she?"

"Not far. Are you ready to meet her?"

"Of course! But... I don't know if she will want to meet *me*," she said, her voice filled with fear.

"She will. She told me so herself."

"You've seen her? You've talked to her about me? Oh my God! Piotr, what do I do now?" she panicked.

She, a master of high-stakes negotiations, was simply afraid—terrified of meeting her own daughter, even though she knew it was inevitable.

"What am I going to say to her? Piotr, what do I say?"

"Nothing. She already knows everything. It was your daughter who found you, not the other way around."

"Did you tell her about me?"

"Not exactly," he paused, then added, "You told her yourself."

"Piotr, stop it, this is no time for jokes."

"Can I call her in now?"

"Is she here?" Joanna asked, her voice suddenly calm as she guessed that Piotr had brought her.

"Yes, she's waiting outside the door until I prepare you for the meeting."

"Ask her to come in, and then please leave us. I'd like to be alone with her."

"Fine, but that won't be necessary, I assure you."

She looked at him in surprise, not understanding what he meant.

"I only had to prepare *you* for this meeting," he explained. "Your daughter didn't need any preparation; she discovered everything herself."

"How is that possible?" she interrupted.

"She'll tell you herself. You've known each other before, but you were unaware of who the other was," he added as he walked to the door and opened it.

"Come in. Your mother is waiting," they heard him say to someone in the hallway.

CHAPTER VII
GHAZNI BASE

The repair base in Ghazni was the focal point for all the mechanical failures plaguing the military equipment stationed at forward operating bases. But it wasn't just vehicles mangled by IEDs or transporters with sinister, hard-to-diagnose issues that ended up here. A significant portion of the incoming transport consisted of functional, or nearly functional, vehicles from their own troops. To keep everything operational, they needed the golden hands of their mechanics, their expertise, and a vast supply of spare parts.

This was the biggest problem. On paper, the logistics looked perfectly normal. Minor repairs and routine maintenance were handled on-site, with full inspections conducted according to regulations and standard operating procedures. Anything that couldn't be repaired locally, yet was still deemed salvageable from a cost perspective, was shipped back to Poland to be handled by Senator G...'s company.

So where is the heart of this corruption? wondered Captain Kowalczyk, who had been delegated to investigate how a 20 kg package of cocaine had ended up in a shipping container in Gdynia. He had been sitting at this base for three months, and his primary discovery was that all the bureaucrats and soldiers involved in training future officers had surprisingly free access to the local civilian population.

That's where the drugs are coming from, he concluded from his investigation so far. They're brought onto the base and loaded for shipment.

There was a second possibility—a transfer point somewhere between the repair base and the airport where the equipment was flown out. Drugs could also be hidden during the loading process onto the transport planes. However, most equipment was sent to Poland via shipping containers, and Kowalczyk was certain this was the primary smuggling route.

Captain Kowalczyk himself was a mysterious figure. His appointment to the 7th rotation of troops had surprised the tight-knit group of soldiers sent to Afghanistan. After months of joint exercises and training, most of them knew each other well and worked cohesively. While still in Poland, he had analyzed the military files of all personnel who could be connected to the drug scandal. His four-person team had initially identified eight suspects. Three served in Warsaw, while the rest were stationed right here at the Ghazni base.

The threads of their mutual connections and prior service all converged at a Pomeranian garrison, where they had known each other at various times, having all trained together. As often happens in military careers, their paths had diverged, but the fact that three of them now held staff positions with direct influence over personnel assignments kept the captain awake at night.

He had examined their financial records and determined, beyond a doubt, that they all possessed assets far exceeding what their military salaries could explain. In itself, this wasn't a crime, but it was a glaring red flag.

Lost in thought, Kowalczyk left his office, located in the last logistics barracks nestled against a wall of sandbags protecting the facility from rocket fire from the nearby hills. He headed towards the building housing the canteen and communications stations. Dust coated every exposed part of his skin, and his sunglasses did little to protect his eyes, serving more to let him observe passing soldiers without betraying his interest.

In the left pocket of his combat shirt, his hand clenched around a copy of a mysterious note that had been slipped to him during a visit to the bathhouse. After a shower, he had gotten dressed and found the note, written in Dari—one of Afghanistan's official languages—in his pocket.

Its contents drilled into his mind, making him realize the danger here was very real, and it wasn't just from the Taliban, but potentially from the Polish soldiers he served alongside. He might have even shared a meal with them, laughed at their jokes, and listened to their stories from trips outside the wire.

The most puzzling aspect was the method the sender had used. There was no doubt it was a warning. The Dari text seemed like it came from an online translator or had been deliberately distorted by a local interpreter to mislead him about the author's identity.

...Your arms are too long and you may lose them. Your breath will grow shorter and shorter until it is lost completely in the shadows around you. Return to your mother and the land of friendly souls, so your flesh does not rot in these sands. All that is pure is subject to Allah, and you are not His servant, nor are you a law for us. Let His servants live, and you yourself will survive...

He had sent the original note back to Poland for analysis, but they found nothing—no fingerprints, no other traces. The only clue was that the A4 paper was manufactured in Poland, and the printer used was of American origin, with no record of any official correspondence from their database being printed on it.

He had shared the news with the only person who knew his true purpose here: Lieutenant Tomasz Karolak, a young mechanic. Karolak was an exceptional intelligence gatherer. His analytical mind and unique ability to gain people's trust earned him as many friends as it did enemies. A fabricated resume and false certifications had paved his way into a position at Senator G...'s "Smith Small Repair Plant," from where, after six months of work under military supervision, he was deployed to the Ghazni base.

Karolak sat heavily in his chair and checked his watch. The captain was ten minutes late. He narrowed his eyes, avoiding the gaze of the two colonels at the next table. What he had discovered today had electrified him. He knew it was a breakthrough in the case, and they had to act immediately. The metaphorical bomb was already ticking; the threat was no longer abstract but very real.

"Where the hell have you been?" he hissed as Kowalczyk finally sat down at his table with infuriating calm.

"What happened?" the captain replied evenly, casting a meaningful glance at the nearby soldiers.

"Let's go," was all Karolak said. He stood up and moved toward the exit. The fact that the two men were known to be friends was no secret; it couldn't be hidden. This was a calculated part of their operational cover, designed to make their meetings seem innocuous.

They weaved through the hall, watched by several soldiers. Holding a bottle of beer, Tomasz led them toward the noisy arcade game machines. *The sound from these cabinets will drown out our words,* he thought, turning to face Kowalczyk.

"This morning, I overheard a conversation," Tomasz began cautiously.

"Go on."

Tomasz scanned their surroundings. Seeing no one nearby, he noted the security camera in the corner and turned his back to it. A lip-reading specialist could decipher everything they said, so he was careful.

"Major Zenon K... He's involved in this," he whispered quietly, his eyes fixed on the machine's screen where colorful graphics flashed and jumped noisily.

Kowalczyk pulled the lever on his own machine, setting it in motion.

"They're interested in you. They want to stage an accident. They're afraid you've discovered something that's right under your nose, something to do with the drugs and the equipment repairs. Have you recently reviewed any documents related to the last shipment of machines sent for overhaul?" Tomasz asked.

"I'm always reviewing something. Tell me what you heard," Kowalczyk replied after a moment's thought.

"I was in the specialist ready-room. I eavesdropped on everything happening in the office of the Deputy Commander of the Polish Military Contingent (DPSZ)."

The captain glanced sideways at Tomasz, who continued his report with a calm demeanor. Kowalczyk was acutely aware that this was the first time Tomasz had revealed he had the operational capability to surveil and eavesdrop on the office of the base's supreme commander.

Does he have official authorization for this? he thought for a moment. *But who would grant it? A court? Or his CBA superiors?* The reflection came to him a second later. He knew Tomasz was with the Central Anticorruption Bureau, and that's where the answers lay.

Is he testing me? A thought ran through his head. Or is he genuinely trying to protect me?

"They want to get rid of the evidence," Tomasz continued. "They know the drug seizure in Gdynia could lead investigators right to them. The colonel was talking to someone at Headquarters in Warsaw. Unfortunately, he didn't use any names."

"'You have to sever all contacts and get rid of every inconvenient person immediately, otherwise heads will roll— and I mean at the highest level. This is an order,' the person on the other end said."

"'And I'll take care of the ones here personally,' I heard our Chief reply."

"Then there was silence. Our Chief confirmed he would be in Poland for a meeting of the General Staff, where they would 'determine what and how.' Of course, from Poland, I might be able to identify who he was talking to, but it's impossible to trace from here."

A one-armed bandit nearby rang a bell, imitating a win. The machines only paid out in points; there was no real money to be squeezed from them, so over time, interest had waned, and only a few enthusiasts still wasted time pulling the metal handles.

Tomasz walked away from the machine and slowly approached the bar.

"One more beer, please," he said to a young corporal standing behind the counter.

He returned to the vending machine area.

"I'm going back to Poland," Kowalczyk said, his voice low. "I can't do anything more here. There definitely won't be another shipment anytime soon, and I'll find out more on the ground. Let me know if you come across anything else. And watch your back." He turned his gaze toward Tomasz. "Contact me through the usual channels," he added, his eyes fixed on the three horizontal cherries displayed behind the machine's window.

Tomasz nodded in understanding.

"It's you who needs to be careful," he replied, patting Kowalczyk on the back. He watched him walk away with a sense of foreboding. He didn't even want to admit to himself that he'd grown to like the man.

"A lack of emotion is fundamental to this work," his instructor's words rang in his ears. But were nascent friendships considered negative emotions? He still hadn't found an answer.

Meanwhile, Kowalczyk turned on his heel, placed his empty bottle on a counter, and walked calmly—without looking from side to side—toward the hallway where he stored his weapon. He quickly strapped on a bulletproof vest, threw a sweatshirt over it, and stepped out of the building.

The walk to his quarters felt longer than usual. Scanning his surroundings carefully, he walked down the middle of the wide road, occasionally passing stragglers or soldiers hurrying to their posts. He knew he had been assigned protection, but he didn't know who his "guardians" were. Their role was to watch over him discreetly. Here, in a place where everyone carried firearms and had access to other dangerous explosives, providing close protection was extremely difficult. It consisted mainly of identifying potential threats and gathering intelligence wherever possible, particularly among the local Afghan helpers. It was an open secret that they had a fondness for Washington's green banknotes. Here, everyone could be corrupted—from translators to the police who cooperated with them, to other officials in the Afghan administration. And they often were.

Buying twenty kilograms of hashish was no problem for them. The challenge was getting the merchandise onto the base and then shipping it to Poland. The military police cordon protecting the base was practically airtight and impossible for an ordinary soldier to breach. This wasn't about the small, personal-use quantities of drugs that some soldiers smuggled in; they didn't concern themselves with that. It wasn't what they were sent here to investigate.

Kowalczyk was thinking more deeply than usual, a habit he'd suppressed during his deployment. His mind raced, trying to piece together how the massive profits from the drug trade were being divided among those who provided the protective umbrella over the entire operation.

CHAPTER VIII
MYSTERY

Joanna stood frozen in surprise as she watched the door slowly open. A slender, pretty figure stepped across the threshold, her face completely hidden behind a huge bouquet of daffodils—Joanna's favorite flower. She held them as if ashamed to reveal herself.

"Hello, Mom... I guess I can call you that now?" a familiar voice asked.

The flowers lowered, revealing a face Joanna knew well.

The girl approached and, handing over the bouquet, asked with a tremor in her voice, "Won't you hug your daughter? ...Mommy."

That single word—"Mommy"—spurred her into action.

"Piotr!" she shouted after him, but he was already closing the door behind him.

"And I told you I had no reason to leave," his voice came from the other side. "Say hello, Joasia. She really is your daughter."

Only then did she believe him. Bursting into tears, she threw her arms around Aśka. She hugged and kissed her, repeating one word over and over: "Forgive me... forgive me, my little girl."

"Mom, I have nothing to forgive you for. Please, stop blaming yourself."

"I'm so happy... I'm so very happy," Aśka said as they both sank onto the sofa, holding each other.

"My mother—the one who raised me—died two weeks ago," Aśka began, and then she too broke down in tears.

Now they were both sobbing in each other's arms.

"But I have you, and you have me," Aśka continued, her voice thick with emotion.

Piotr brought them glasses of water and then sat quietly in an armchair, waiting. He knew a torrent of questions was about to begin. Joanna was too pragmatic not to want every detail. *Aśka inherited that trait from her,* he thought.

When they had finally shed a "sea of tears," they composed themselves and turned to Piotr. Joanna asked the inevitable question: "How is this possible?"

"It *is* possible, Joanna. Believe me," he replied, glancing at Aśka, who was still accustomed to treating Joanna as a client and hadn't yet shifted to a more familiar tone. "Aśka will tell you everything. This meeting is her doing."

"Please, tell me. I don't understand any of this," Joanna said, turning to Aśka.

Piotr, who had prepared earlier, now opened the champagne.

"First, a toast," he said, filling their glasses. "To a happy reunion, and to the fact that sitting here with us is your second daughter... and your sister, Aśka."

They drank. Then Aśka began to speak.

"When my mother fell ill—please don't be angry that I call her that, but I have all my life, and I still feel that way. May I still speak of her like that?"

"Just try not to," Joanna joked softly. "I've been waiting for this for so many years," she added, her voice full of emotion.

"So, my mother, as she was dying, told me that the child she gave birth to had died. And that she had switched me with the baby girl lying next to her in the hospital. She swapped the identification bands on our wrists. So after two days, I went home with her as her daughter. No one knew, not even her husband. Only Mrs. Genia, a friend of my mother's who was a midwife there, guessed the truth. My mother worked as a nurse in the surgical ward, and the two were friends. At my mother's funeral, I approached Mrs. Genia—whom I knew well—and she looked at me through her tears and asked, 'Did she tell you the truth?'

'Yes,' I said.

Then we spoke honestly. Mrs. Genia knew that the young girl's baby—you, Joanna—was going to be given up for adoption. She had told my mother about it before you gave birth.

'You know,' she told my mother then, 'she's been through a terrible tragedy. Her mother cries constantly in the hallway and has to compose herself before she goes in. She once confided in me that the baby would be adopted because her daughter was relinquishing her rights.'

When you unexpectedly gave birth to twins, you held them only once and cut locks of their hair, sobbing. 'This is for my daughter,' you said to the midwife, Mrs. Genia, who watched in surprise. You didn't know that one of those girls had already been swapped."

"It was possible because the doctor examining the newborns was exhausted—three deliveries at once after an all-night duty, including one very difficult birth. He had to save a young girl's life and give her a transfusion because she had lost too much blood during the twin delivery. So when he diagnosed a very serious heart defect in one of the girls immediately after birth, he was terrified. In his carelessness, he mistook my mother's child for the child of the girl lying behind the screen, the one receiving a blood transfusion. All three baby girls on the table at that time looked very similar; they all had blond hair."

"He filled out the sick baby's chart, listing you, Joanna, as the mother and giving her a very low Apgar score. But the identification band on that baby's wrist was mine. So my mother had to switch them back. She did it herself. Neither my mother nor Mrs. Genia corrected the doctor at the time, even though they knew the very sick infant was my mother's biological daughter, not yours. You, Joanna, were that girl, the one who was so ill and deeply depressed."

"My adoptive mother's biological daughter died soon after. No one told you; they were afraid for you, given your fragile state. And Mrs. Genia remained silent all these years, fearful for her job and my mother's."

"Finding confirmation in the hospital files and other documents wasn't so difficult after that. I started by checking my blood type against my adoptive parents'. I couldn't be their biological child. When I found your full name and your date of delivery in the hospital records, everything became clear. It was all true. Everything matched perfectly. I also found a death certificate for a baby girl—my adoptive mother's biological daughter. Only then did I understand why my mother constantly went to the cemetery, searching for a grave. She never found it, but I will find it. I have to do that for her," she added.

"There's something else," Aśka said after a moment of silence.

"What?" Piotr and Joanna asked in unison.

"My name. Everyone calls me Aśka, but my real name is Joanna. My adoptive mother gave me your name. She knew it."

"You already know the rest. But there's one more thing I need to do," she said, turning to Joanna. "Mom—may I ask you for a pair of scissors?" she asked, her tone playful yet utterly serious.

"They're in the bathroom, dear," Joanna replied.

Aśka stood up, spinning in place, unsure where to go. There was no obvious door to the bathroom.

"Come, I'll show you. My house is your home," Joanna said, leading her toward the hidden door in the bookcase.

A moment later, Aśka returned with the scissors.

Piotr understood instantly what she intended to do. She didn't have to—he had already secretly checked. As soon as he suspected Aśka's true parentage, he had collected hairs from both Joanna and Aśka and sent them for DNA analysis. He had received the results two days prior: *"A 99.9% genetic match confirms a mother-daughter relationship."* He couldn't have told Joanna he had found her daughter without being absolutely certain. This test was the final proof; Aśka had not been wrong.

He watched her but remained silent, a knowing smile playing on his lips. Joanna noticed the smile but misinterpreted it.

What does she want to do, my little girl? The term felt strange yet wonderful in her mind.

Aśka took a strand of her own hair and cut off a sizable lock.

"Please," she said, handing it to Joanna. "Check the DNA."

"You don't have to! I believe you!" Joanna hastily assured her. A part of her was afraid of the test—*what if Piotr and Aśka had made a mistake?* The disturbing thought flashed through her mind.

"Faith alone isn't enough, Mom. We have to be sure. Right, Piotr?" she said, turning to him for support.

"I'm sure," he replied truthfully. "But Aśka is right. Check it for yourself."

Joanna took the lock of Aśka's hair with a reverent touch. *I will check it. I have to be certain, too,* she thought.

"Alright, as you wish," she said aloud, moving toward the phone.

"Don't outsource it. Do it yourself," Aśka requested.

Joanna stepped back and hugged her tightly. "I'm so glad I have such a smart daughter."

But that's not your merit, Aśka thought, her mind on the woman who raised her. *It was she who shaped me.* But she said nothing. Why reopen old wounds? None of this was Joanna's fault.

"And what about my hair?" Piotr joked, though his tone held a serious undercurrent.

Both women turned toward him in unison.

They do look a bit alike, he thought, studying their faces. But does Aśka look like me?

CHAPTER IX CATASTROPHE

On Saturday morning, Aśka got into a company van and set off towards Warsaw. Two counterintelligence officers were riding with her. She had to hurry to reach the repair plant in Mały Kovel before noon. She had an appointment there with one of their employees - engineer Jurkiewicz. When they arrived in the town, she sent him a text message.

"I'll be at the market near the fountain in ten minutes. A black van with Gdynia license plates," she added.

She passed a row of low buildings on the right, surrounded by a high concrete fence with a dense tangle of barbed wire at the top. It was a huge plant employing a third of the local residents. Senator G. cared. He knew that the policy of providing great social privileges to his employees guaranteed him a senate seat, which, in turn, allowed him to run several shady businesses.

"Who the hell is this mysterious engineer?" she thought while waiting for him.

The two counterintelligence officers had already gotten out of the car and were securing the area from nearby. A short, stocky man came out of a side alley and began to look around.

Through the van's black tinted window, she saw a man entering the market square, holding their distinguishing mark - a blue briefcase - in his hand.

"He's coming from the direction of the bread shop," she said into the receiver embedded in a small button on her blouse.

The two counterintelligence officers turned their heads unhurriedly towards him.

She stood up and turned on the camera, which was hidden in the mirror housing above the driver's head.

Waiting for the side door of the van to open, she smoothed her hair and pulled up her short skirt, which revealed her long, shapely legs.

He got in unhurriedly and slumped on the seat on the other side of the van.

"Hello, Miss," he said in a voice accustomed to giving orders, and there was something in his tone that made her more vigilant. She was not afraid of a physical attack from him, but rather of some kind of trick. "Maybe he wants to frame me for something?" she thought.

"What do you have for me?" she asked.

"The plans," he replied curtly.

"What do you do in the Senator's company?"

"Protecting military secrets?" His eyes quickly scanned the entire interior of the van.

He handed her the blue briefcase. "Take a look in there as soon as you can."

"Who do you work for?"

"Turn off the microphone," he replied.

"I can't."

"If I say what you'd like to hear, I might not live to tell about it. A voice is as recognizable as a face."

She stood up and turned it off.

"For state intelligence. The secret department has only four people. I report directly to my superior, a Colonel, let's call him X—this is unofficial—and officially to the Military Technical Works. The army's direct superior for them is General Z."

He fell silent, as if weighing his words.

"I discovered that he has ties to Senator G... On his orders, from time to time a special courier, Lieutenant Colonel S..., delivers about half a million zlotys to him by military transport. To be shared, of course. It's he who distributes the money to everyone involved in this scheme."

"What scheme?"

"Don't pretend you don't know. I read your article, and I looked into the rest at your newspaper's editorial office.

That's why you're here. I also got a tip from Skowronek. They wanted to kill him too, and now they're trying to get rid of me as well. But that's not why I contacted you."

"Why, then?"

"I suspect an assassination is being planned."

"Yes," she tried to mask her satisfaction. This was the second source of information about the attack, this time physical and tangible.

"Who? When and where?" She pretended not to know anything.

"Not 'what,' but 'who,'" he corrected her.

"What do you know about this?"

"Far too little," he replied in a slightly disappointed voice. "An analysis of various unrelated events shows that this is a well-thought-out operation to eliminate troublesome people. The first serious signal was the information that all the people involved in this operation were deliberately gathered in one place at the same time. For now, only military personnel. The day after tomorrow, the Air Force Staff is gathering all of them at a special Conference on Securing Military Missions in Afghanistan. The reason for convening this conference was the discovery of drug smuggling from Afghanistan."

Aśka felt satisfied; at last, Skowronek's findings were confirmed by a second, independent source.

"Second, there was a very strange order issued a few days ago to have them all gather on one plane. The plane was treated as a taxi to pick up all the conference participants from across Poland and deliver them to their home bases. At the same time, they changed the pilots and flight dispatchers to less experienced ones, and the selected airports aren't equipped with ILS." After a moment, he explained the abbreviation: "That's a modern system for guiding planes during landing. But the most important piece of evidence is the fact that the main participant of this conference, General Z, isn't flying with them."

"Where did this information come from?"

"I get information from various sources, but the main source is Karolina and General Z's personal computer..."

"Who is Karolina?"

"You have everything in this blue briefcase."

"Why don't you notify the proper authorities?"

"I did. I informed my superior."

"So what?"

"They tried to kill me yesterday morning. They staged a car accident and had me taken to a military psychiatrist. I escaped from the transport and I'm hiding. General Z... and Senator G... are powerful opponents. Don't underestimate them, either."

"I'm disappearing. Do what you want with this," he said, waving his hand towards the blue briefcase.

"How can I help you?"

"Publish it. Or maybe you have a safe house for a few days?" he asked, moving toward the exit.

Aśka thought of Joanna – only she had her own bodyguards and a safe place to hide for a few days.

"I think we can arrange that, but you have to come with us."

"Then I'll take you up on it." He squeezed into the corner of the van and pulled his hat over his eyes.

"Don't be afraid of them," Aśka said, nodding to the counterintelligence officers. "They're private security."

"No one can be trusted," he grumbled rudely.

"You trusted me."

"I had no choice, and besides, Skowronek vouched for you."

She stood up and turned on the microphone.

"The meeting's over," she said to the counterintelligence officers.

After returning to Gdynia, Piotr held a meeting in the conference room of his office. Everyone involved in the investigation of Senator G... was there: all the counterintelligence officers, the newspaper's editor-in-chief, and a few lawyers.

"We stepped on a landmine, and now we have to defuse it without harming ourselves and our company," said Aśka.

Piotr nodded approvingly at these words.

A silent click came from the projector; it was Aśka presenting another set of documents from the blue briefcase. The editor-in-chief and his two lawyers sat quietly, their eyes wide with amazement.

"These are the originals?" the editor-in-chief asked, straightening up in his chair as if sitting there was a form of torture.

"Yes, at least they look like it."

"Have you read all the documents?"

"No, I didn't have enough time. However, none of this makes sense by normal civilian logic. This kind of reasoning only works in the military or the secret services. Here, the leads hit a dead end, a closed circle of work dependencies and a small group of people. That is the key to this puzzle."

"We need to focus on the assassination tip. Although I don't see anything like that in the documents you've presented," said the editor-in-chief.

"We could use a military man with a background in aviation," muttered the counterintelligence officer.

Only going public with this story quickly can save their skins—as long as all these revelations are true and aren't a provocation intended to destroy your company," suggested one of the editor-in-chief's lawyers. "You've stepped on the toes of many powerful people. This isn't a joke, but a fierce clash with the secret services. Have you considered the consequences?" he asked.

"We think about it all the time," Piotr replied, and to his surprise, he noticed that the Editor-in-Chief was very nervous.

He leaned over to Aśka and whispered, "Did you vet the Chief?"

"Yes, and he's completely clean, but he's a coward," she replied quietly.

"I need a ten-minute break," the Editor-in-Chief requested.

Everyone left, leaving the two of them alone. The brainstorming session had been organized here at the Company specifically for him, because it would be impossible to keep it secret at the newspaper office.

To an outside observer, the large conference table filled with documents might have seemed like a mess. However, this was not the case; everything was organized for the Editor-in-Chief and his team of lawyers, who now, bent over the documents, looked like a panel of experts trying to quickly answer test questions.

"We are printing tomorrow. Will we be on time?" Aśka asked the Editor-in-Chief.

"The Senator and the General will be embarrassed when they read the paper; it's all there. They are not omnipotent, just cleverly camouflaged, exploiting the legal loopholes in our military tender system."

"What about the assassination theory?"

"I think the evidence for that is too weak, but perhaps we lack the expertise to be sure. Notify the Police and the Prosecutor's Office, and let the relevant authorities handle it and verify it themselves," he decided.

"They have little time; they won't be able to check and verify these claims."

"But they can ground the plane. Try to intervene with the Police Commander," Piotr said, turning to the Editor-in-Chief. "You have the best chance of getting this warning through."

"I don't believe any of this assassination talk. There's no evidence, only speculation. I won't make a fool of myself."

"But there are emails from General Z's computer...."

"That's not enough. There's nothing in them suggesting he's planning an assassination. Send someone to the airport to make sure they don't take off."

"What do you mean, 'someone'? Only Piotr or I can go," Aśka said to the Chief, her voice angry.

"I'll go," Piotr declared, spinning in his chair, volunteering to relieve Aśka.

Later that afternoon—Okęcie Airport. A Hercules stood by the hangar, waiting for its passengers. On the tarmac next to the left wing stood four pilots: the aircraft commander, his co-pilot, and two technicians—one for loading and the other for airframe systems.

They were in no hurry; they had some time before the six passengers from the Military Repair Base arrived.

"How did civilians get permission to fly?" Major Rawadzki, the flight technician, asked his older colleague.

"It's simple—I have an order here from a General in the Polish Military Contingent in Afghanistan. I don't care who I'm flying or where; I'm used to this military taxi service. It's not cheap, but it's convenient for them."

"Damn, and I can't get a refund for my train ticket home later."

"They're here," the co-pilot observed, seeing the Military Police escorting two black government sedans. The cars drove up to the plane unhurriedly. From the first one emerged the portly silhouette of a man with a young girl; from the second, four men in black suits hurriedly got out.

"Those are important people from the Repair Base, and the portly one is Senator G...," the Major informed them.

The pilots went inside before the passengers approached the rear of the plane under the lowered ramp. However, for some reason, the crew did not initiate the system check that would warn them of the plane's proximity to the ground, only glancing at the instruments.

The co-pilot glanced at the control panels. "The EGPWS system should have reported to the aircraft commander." But it didn't; the system remained disabled for the flight, meaning there would be no voice warnings of impending danger. Major Zenon K...'s plan was in motion.

"Everyone to their stations," the aircraft commander instructed the crew via intercom.

The flight technician checked the pre-flight checklist, then briefly instructed everyone to fasten their seatbelts, turn off their phones, and reviewed the flight plan, stating the destination and estimated arrival time. Meanwhile, the Hercules received takeoff clearance and taxied onto the runway.

"We are beginning the takeoff procedure," the aircraft commander announced to his colleagues.

"Systems are functional," the technician said into the microphone.

"We have clearance for takeoff," the commander heard in his headphones. He sat down and fastened his seatbelt. Soon, he felt the plane lift off the ground and climb steadily.

The thirty-three passengers sat in their seats, engaged in conversation, unaware of the danger gathering over their heads.

The Hercules banked gently onto the left wing and, making a turn, climbed to a cruising altitude of 4,800 meters.

After establishing contact with Air Traffic Control, the commander directed the aircraft toward the military airport in Poznań.

After less than two hours of flight, communication was established with the Approach Controller (APP) at Poznań Airport. The Hercules was vectored by the controller and landed gently on the tarmac. It then taxied to a military hangar, coming to a stop near the area for transport planes. Twelve passengers disembarked at a leisurely pace.

Almost no one paid attention to Zenon K..., a Major in the Air Force, a mechanic from the Poznań airport, returning to his home unit after a three-month Hercules maintenance training course in Warsaw.

His nervous gaze and hurried movements did not escape the attention of Karolina, an aide to Senator G... She had taken an interest in him when choosing her seat, deliberately sitting next to him to make contact. Her job left little time for personal relationships with men, but she was drawn to his aviation uniform and stern, masculine face. She found him handsome, as she liked strong, determined types. Within just 15 minutes of the flight, she was holding his hand and looking at him flirtatiously, ignoring the curious glances of nearby passengers. After an hour, she followed him into the toilet, where she eagerly threw herself at him, kissing him on the mouth. The thought of sex in the sky aroused her, but he was apparently not as interested; he pushed her away decisively.

"Not here, not now," he whispered, opening the door and leaving the toilet.

Disappointed, she returned to her seat.

"When will you be in Warsaw again?" she asked, sitting back down.

"In two weeks, for a longer stay," he replied, looking into her eyes.

The plane began its descent, so they fastened their seatbelts and waited to land.

"Turn on your cell phone; I'll send you my private number," she said, reaching for her phone.

"I don't have a mobile phone."

"What do you mean?" She looked at him, surprised.

"I lost it," he answered, but his eyes darted upward as if following a fly.

"Oh, wait, I'll give you a business card right now." As she said this, she dropped her phone back into the depths of her purse. She rummaged for a bit and soon handed him her business card from Senator G...'s office.

He barely looked at it before stuffing it into the top pocket of his uniform.

"Call me when you're in Warsaw," she said in a soft, encouraging voice.

"Okay."

"Is that all?" she felt a flash of disappointment.

The plane stopped, and he stood up. He looked at her as if he wanted to say something important, but finally turned and followed the other passengers toward the exit.

"Why is he so nervous?" she wondered. But her attention was immediately captured by Senator G..., who engaged her in a conversation that kept her so busy she forgot to turn on the phone lying at the bottom of her purse.

Thus, Aśka's attempts to call her during the stopover were unsuccessful. There would be no further attempts, leaving only a record of the call with the mobile carrier. After fifteen minutes, and once several passengers had disembarked, the plane took off again, continuing its flight to the military airport in Świnoujście.

Meanwhile, Piotr was speeding toward the airport in Kołobrzeg, where the Hercules was scheduled to make its third stop.

Every agency he had contacted to request the flight be suspended had politely but firmly refused.

"We understand, but there's nothing we can do at this point. You need something concrete."

"But I have nothing concrete, only suspicions," he lamented to the Naval Command in Gdynia.

"If you get something specific, please let us know," said the duty officer at the Ministry of Defense, ending his involvement in the matter.

"Damn it! Maybe I should say there's a bomb on board; then they'll ground the plane," he complained to Aśka over the phone.

"Yes, a good and effective idea, but that comes with a guaranteed 5-year prison sentence. Do you want that?"

"What jerks—as usual, they don't get it."

"Maybe they do, but they have their procedures and won't do anything without direct orders. And what if we're wrong? Go to the airport and try to call Karolina, Senator G...'s aide. I have her number. Give her the code word 'Cleaner'; she'll know it's not a joke and will want to save her own life."

"Where did you get that?"

"Don't ask, just do it. I've been trying, but her phone is off. You still have some time; they've taken off from Poznań but are still landing in Świnoujście, so you should make it."

Piotr arrived at the Kołobrzeg airport twenty minutes before the scheduled landing, as the Hercules was already on its final approach.

In the cockpit:

"PLF zero forty-three, this is Gdańsk FIS," the co-pilot called.

"Gdańsk FIS, this is PLF zero forty-three," the co-pilot responded.

"PLF zero forty-three, you are cleared for FL 080—I repeat, flight level zero eight zero."

After descending to 2,450 meters, the commander contacted the Świnoujście Airport controller.

"Request landing conditions."

A moment later, the air traffic controller's voice came through the cockpit speakers.

"...PLF zero thirty-three, you are cleared to land on course two-two-zero, I repeat two-two-zero degrees. QNH is 820. Current wind three-zero-zero degrees, up to two meters per second. Cloud cover 7/9, base approximately eighty meters, visibility two kilometers."

The reported height of the cloud base was incorrect; the clouds were actually 20 to 30 meters lower. This wasn't yet a disaster, as the flight was proceeding in the clouds anyway. At 17 km from the runway threshold, the crew established contact with the precision approach controller, who, for the first time during this approach, commanded a course change on the glide path. The precision approach controller was unaware that the aircraft was being pushed by a crosswind of about 15 m/s, and he didn't understand why it was happening.

Then there were a number of irregularities. The aircraft crew reported altitude in feet, while the controller used meters. This in itself isn't catastrophic, but it forces the crew to divert their attention to unit conversions instead of focusing on the critical tasks of the landing approach.

The first approach was unsuccessful, and the controller issued a command for a go-around. The pilot initiated a climb at an altitude of about 200 meters (approximately 650 feet) according to the barometric altimeter, and about 175 meters (approximately 575 feet) according to the radio altimeter. He probably wasn't sure whether the crew was calibrating their altitude based on QFE or QNH pressure settings. The fundamental difference is one we'll never be able to figure out now, because the Hercules was not equipped with a cockpit voice recorder.

The aircraft entered a turn, during which it drifted to the right of the approach course. This could have been caused by the controller incorrectly programming the landing course at the initial point of the turn.

Both pilots, straining forward in their seats, were focused on visually locating the runway and its approach lights.

The aircraft began to uncontrollably increase its bank angle while simultaneously losing heading. After exceeding a 40-degree bank, with just 10 seconds left before impact, the aural warning from the hazard system should have activated. However, no alarm sounded because it had been disabled since the start of the flight.

"What the hell is going on!" shouted the Colonel as he burst into the cockpit. A single glance at the artificial horizon indicators was enough. While they showed a relatively level attitude, his fighter pilot instincts weren't fooled; he knew the plane was in a dangerous descent with insufficient power to recover from such a steep bank.

"Level off! Pull up!" he shouted at the stunned Hercules commander.

Karolina, too, was staring with astonished eyes—but at the illuminated screen of her cell phone. Right after turning it on, she had opened a text message from Aśka and read: "Cleaner" – get off the plane – immediately.

At that moment, the plane's left wing clipped the ground. The aircraft spun 180 degrees and slammed into a grassy field. It tumbled twice, shearing off a wing and most of the tail. Seats with the torn bodies of strapped-in passengers were thrown from the ruptured fuselage. The cockpit, crushed flat like a stomped beer can, sank half a meter into the earth and fell silent. Then, fire burst from the right wing, reaching the fuel tanks within seconds and exploding into a pillar of orange flame that shot skyward. A few jagged stumps of felled trees intensified the horror of the scene. It had happened less than half a kilometer from the runway.

From the airport control tower, they saw the towering plumes of fire above a young grove near the airport.

The air traffic controller, without wasting a moment, grabbed the phone and began frantically calling emergency services. Then, using the emergency communication line, he notified the ARCC (Aeronautical Rescue Coordination Center) in Warsaw about the crash. From there, an order was immediately relayed to Darłówowo, scrambling two rescue helicopters that were maintained there in a state of constant readiness.

"OK, I'm close to the Kołobrzeg airport. I hope to stop them and prevent them from flying further, even if I have to drive onto the tarmac," Piotr informed Aśka over the phone, overtaking a truck with considerable bravado. "Where are their other stopovers?"

"After Kołobrzeg, they land in Gdańsk and end in Krakow, but it's unlikely they'll make it there now."

"Why do you say that?"

"Some passengers got off in Poznań," she added.

It took Piotr less than two hours to reach Kołobrzeg. He entered the terminal and headed straight for the security office. He was just explaining the purpose of his visit to the duty officer when the officer, pressing a hand to his earpiece, said:

"Too late. The Hercules just crashed near Świnoujście."

Immediately afterward, the officer signaled to two guards standing nearby.

"Detain him until the police arrive."

On the way to the holding room, Piotr managed to call Aśka.

"They crashed near Świnoujście and they're detaining me for questioning. Do something!"

She did what she could, but they didn't release him immediately. He had to provide a full statement at the Police Headquarters. Only the intervention of the counterintelligence officer he had worked with, combined with a phone call from the editor-in-chief of the "Dziennik

Pomorski," secured his release—though it came with the conditions of signing a statement, a travel ban, and an order to report to the police in Gdynia the next day.

He returned to the office, deeply dejected.

"We did everything we could," Aśka consoled him. "The plane crash proves we were right."

"That's a dubious satisfaction," Piotr replied in a somber tone. "We didn't do everything. We could have saved them."

General Z...'s Office

The General, the Task Force Commander, sat in his office, chin resting on his hand. He stared with tired eyes at the TV screen, where every channel had been showing the burning wreckage of the Hercules for several minutes. The commentary from reporters on the scene was unanimous and critical of the army. The recurring question was about the presence of nearly the entire command elite of a Polish Army division on a single plane. How could so many senior commanders be allowed to travel together? How could a modern transport plane just crash?

"It was an assassination!" thundered right-wing channels and the political opposition, after receiving information that someone had tried to halt the flight.

"He did it. The motherf***er actually did it, even though I forbade him." The General felt things had slipped from his grasp. "This is what happens when you use amateurs," he thought, recalling his conversation with the Major. He surmised that the permanent disconnection and jamming of the artificial horizon indicators had been effectively handled by Major Zenon K.—the brother of a Wolverine driver killed in Afghanistan.

"Gregory!" he barked.

Captain J... entered the office.

"Summon all the subordinate commanders from the Transport Aviation Regiment, and those who disembarked from the Hercules earlier, for a meeting tomorrow," he ordered his adjutant.

Meanwhile, two logistics company commanders, the officer for the KTO (Wheeled Armored Personnel Carrier) Rosomak program, and the director of the Repair Base—all involved in overseeing equipment overhauls for Afghanistan—had already arrived in his office.

The General sat in silence; he was visibly deeply affected by the crash. He waited for everyone to take their seats at the conference table.

"All critical issues regarding the potential cause of this crash must be addressed here and now," General Z... began. "I've already received a call from the Military Prosecutor's Office. They are demanding we make available everyone who had a direct or indirect role in preparing the flight and its departure."

Colonel Ludwisiak listened in silence to the General's words. It was me who authorized civilians on that Hercules flight yesterday morning. It was against regulations, but you can't refuse the Senator... he's the General's man. And now he's probably going to pin this on me. He mentally scanned his actions, searching for any traces of their collaboration. The trail was clear—a courier brought him cash every month. Damn, how am I going to explain this? But, maintaining a calm tone, he continued his train of thought, looking pointedly at General Z...

"Senator G... died in the crash, along with many innocent people. I believe he's connected to this catastrophe, because I'm convinced it wasn't an accident. What about N.J., Senator G...'s right-hand man?" Colonel Ludwisiak began cautiously. "He's the only other person who knew all of us. While the Senator assured me N.J. knew nothing, I don't believe it. But that's not the worst of it," he assured them.

"Then what is?" the General asked in an irritated tone.

"An article in the *Gazeta Pomorska*. Don't any of you know about it?" His piercing gaze scanned everyone at the table.

They didn't. They had been preoccupied with the catastrophe and had missed the news reports that had appeared that morning, which were otherwise dominated by accounts of the Hercules crash.

"Who is behind it?" the General demanded, as the others remained silent, afraid to voice their opinions.

"You are," stated their specialist in rigging tenders.

The General stiffened, then violently jumped up from the table. He fixed Captain Dębski with a steely gaze, but it made no impression. The Captain also stood up, approached the still-standing General, and looked at the screen of his laptop. With astonished eyes, he read what appeared to be pre-prepared answers to potential questions from the Prosecutor's Office, which was set to interrogate them.

"May I?" the Captain asked. "A thought just occurred to me. For two months, I've been wondering how information about our meetings was leaking to outsiders."

He glanced at the General's laptop again.

"You have your internet connection on, correct?" His tone suggested a statement rather than a question.

The General gave a silent nod.

The Captain took a step back, reached into his briefcase, and pulled out a small device. He plugged it into his own laptop and watched the screen. A series of green pulses in the shape of sine waves began to form a significant graph on the display.

"You're being targeted. You have spyware. Within hours, everything you type here will be sent to whoever planted it—a high-class hacker, or someone from the special services," he told the General.

The General snatched up the laptop with undisguised rage and slammed it against the edge of the table. The device shattered into two pieces.

"I warned you all. So? We're fucked! They have everything you wrote in there. You've sunk us all!" he yelled.

"Who has it?" The General's resigned voice made everyone acutely aware of the danger.

The Captain was convinced a rival group, composed of former intelligence operatives, was behind it. "Given everything they've already published about us, we have to assume we're already in their crosshairs. We need to start covering our tracks. Our biggest liability was Senator G..., and now that he's gone..." He paused for a moment. "...but N.J., his business partner, is still out there. Who's going to handle that?" he asked, slowly looking at each of them.

Silence was his answer.

"What do you mean?" Colonel Ludwisiak asked a foolish question.

Kowalczyk let it go. It's hopeless. I'm not going to explain the obvious, he thought, and besides, I need to be careful. Corruption is one thing, but inciting murder is another.

After a moment of silence in the room, he spoke again.

"You also need to deal with this hacker and the journalist who's on our trail, and fast."

"Where is he getting this information?" the Plant Director dared to ask.

"I'm not sure, but I suspect it came from the Senator. He was our weakest link. All this scrutiny started with the drugs found in the Rosomak."

There's a grim logic to it, the General thought. A surprise we never could have anticipated in our wildest assumptions.

"We need to get ahead of them," General Z... picked up the thread, addressing the others. "We'll call a press conference to divert attention away from us. We cannot risk losing the trust of our superiors—that would be the end of us."

"That's all clear, but how do you plan to achieve it?"

"The usual playbook: blame xenophobic civilians within the special services. We'll suggest this is their provocation to oust the current Minister of Defence. We'll ride this scandal, and the Hercules catastrophe can help us significantly."

"Who's going to do it?" Dębski asked.

"You'd be the best fit, but your rank is too low. It has to be one of the colonels."

"A conspiracy theory could work," noted the previously silent Colonel Ludwisiak.

"Good, you'll lead the conference. Get ready. You have three hours."

His voice was regaining confidence. They knew him and his mood swings, from utter resignation to unfounded optimism.

"You," he turned his head towards the silent Director, "will go to your office and destroy any documents that could lead investigators to us."

"There are no such documents," the Director retorted indignantly.

"Check everything again—from faxes and call logs to your department managers' notes."

"Fine," he nodded, acquiescing.

"Dismissed," the General said firmly to those present.

As the Colonel was leaving, the General patted him on the shoulder. "You can do this," he assured him.

"Stay," he said to Captain Dębski.

When they were alone, the General looked at him intently. "You're right," he began, with a new emphasis in his voice, "but it doesn't change the fact that we need a different approach, or it's the end for us. Do you know Major Zenon K...? He's our solution. You point him at a target, and he eliminates it. It will be expensive, but we have no choice.

There's no one left to provide the off-the-books income we've all grown accustomed to."

The Captain smiled ironically.

"I got the least of it," he noted.

"This is no time to argue. The Major should be directed to remove the remaining obstacles and then become the scapegoat for this whole affair. Understood? It has to look like his personal act of revenge," he added, looking cynically into his eyes.

The Captain stood up, walked over to the coffee machine, and poured himself a cup. *"What does he expect from me? He wants me to agree to murder,"* he recalled his earlier fears.

"It's not a very smart idea," he remarked, drumming his fingers nervously on the table.

"Why not?"

"Other criminal statutes," he replied. "Besides, I'm not sure anyone will even get to the truth. I'm convinced it will all be swept under the rug."

"Unfortunately, I don't have the same influence I used to," the General added in a resigned voice. The times when he was respected were over. Now he wanted only one thing: to get out of this alive, at any cost, even if it meant a dishonorable discharge. Zenon K... was his last chance before a "bullet of honor."

"Alright," the Captain said unexpectedly, "give me his contact." He agreed because he had conceived an intrigue that, if successful, would clear him of all suspicion and keep him out of prison.

After receiving the password and email for Major Zenon K..., the Captain sat down at the general's computer and sent him a message using General Z...'s login credentials. *The game is afoot. Now we just have to wait for the first move*, he thought with satisfaction.

The phone rang. The General picked up. "Yes, Mr. Prosecutor," the Captain heard before he slipped out of the office, leaving the General in a foul mood acquired from the prosecutor's call.

The Captain returned to his desk two floors up and sat down at his computer. He composed a cryptographically encrypted text and sent it to the Chief Military Prosecutor's address. In it, he briefly described the task the General had given him, listed the names of everyone involved, and offered his full cooperation in exchange for crown witness status.

Now he relaxed. The worst was behind him. What lay ahead was a big question mark.

However, he hadn't foreseen everything. He couldn't have known about Colonel Ludwisiak's weak nerves.

"Conference tomorrow at noon at the Headquarters." That was the only message sent to journalists from the Colonel's office.

From the very next morning, the Colonel was preparing for the meeting with journalists in the large briefing room. He was tormented by contradictory feelings: loyalty, submission, and professional dependence on his superior on one hand, and the screaming instinct of self-preservation on the other—*Save yourself!*

He had just received an encrypted text from his contact in the Military Prosecutor's Office:

CASE OF THE CRASH REASSIGNED TO THE NATIONAL PROSECUTOR'S OFFICE UNDER SUPERVISION OF MINISTER OF DEFENCE - STOP.

INTERVENTION BY CHIEF OF GENERAL STAFF UNSUCCESSFUL - STOP.

WOLVERINES AT MILITARY POLICE ATTENTION CENTER IN POZNAŃ - STOP.

BE CAREFUL - STOP.

The pensive Colonel was interrupted by Captain W..., his spokesman—assigned to him by General Z...'s order—who handed him the freshly written statement.

"What are you doing?" asked Captain W...

"Nothing. I'm going off-script," the Colonel replied. "Let them in."

The Captain left the Colonel for a moment and quickly disappeared through another door. He entered his office and dialed a number from his double-encrypted phone.

"He tore up the statement—what are your orders?" he inquired.

After a pause.

"Understood. But it's a big risk."

"Orders confirmed," he repeated before hanging up.

He passed the Corporal guarding the entrance to the meeting room and disappeared into the technical rooms.

The Corporal let the journalists and reporters from the vestibule into the room. For the next ten minutes, the room was a chaos of cameras, microphones, and the noise of conversation. When the Colonel stood up and asked for silence, the chatter and shuffling of chairs slowly subsided. Captain W... sat down next to him at the table and took a microphone.

"Quiet, please!" his voice echoed through the room. "Colonel Ludwisiak has convened a press conference regarding yesterday's press publications about alleged irregularities in the overhaul of military equipment in Afghanistan."

"The floor is yours, Colonel," he said, placing the microphone on the tripod and waiting for the Colonel's words.

The Colonel suddenly felt his courage and reason desert him. He took the microphone in his hand, and at that moment, a violent convulsion wracked his body. He collapsed onto the desk, his body twitching. The chair he kicked flew backward, hitting a wall.

At first, there was silence in the room, then loud screams of terror, amplified by the live microphones. TV cameras broadcast the scene to the studios of numerous stations.

Captain W... was the first to react. He jumped up and tugged at the microphone cable on the floor. It was useless; there was too much slack. He pulled it with all his might, but it caught on a leg of the conference table. The Corporal in the corridor heard the noise and screams and rushed into the room. He looked around in alarm and, seeing the Colonel still convulsing on the table, pushed through the journalists in his way. He grabbed the cable right next to the Colonel's hand, which was clenched around the metal handle of the microphone, and pulled hard. The hand holding the microphone jerked toward him, but fell a few centimeters short, maintaining its deadly grip. A strong jerk tore the cables from the handle, sending the end whipping toward the Corporal. It hissed past his head and hit the wall. There was a crack, and the lights went out, plunging the room into darkness, illuminated only by the pale glow from two windows on the opposite wall.

Two journalists rushed toward the now motionless Colonel. "A doctor!" one of them shouted quickly.

The rest of the reporters continued filming the entire event as if nothing had happened.

"Hyenas," the Corporal snarled at the sight.

Captain W... and the Corporal immediately began CPR and rescue breathing, continuing their efforts until a doctor arrived. They took turns trying to restore his heartbeat and breathing, but without success.

The doctor, who arrived fifteen minutes later, pronounced him dead.

Two hours later, General Z..., watching the news report, muttered to himself: "Two left."

The prosecutor who arrived with the doctor confirmed to the journalists gathered outside that the prosecutor's office was conducting a serious investigation into criminal activity within the Polish Army.

"I cannot tell you anything about the press conference or the issues that were to be raised there. Please direct those questions to Colonel Ludwisiak's superiors."

This was followed by a series of strange official statements suggesting the Colonel had convened the conference without his superiors' knowledge, and no one knew what he had intended to discuss.

They may not know, but I do, thought Aśka, sitting in Joanna's residence for the third day.

That morning, a short, laconic message had arrived in her mailbox at the Editorial Office:

YOU WERE RIGHT. I INVITE YOU TO A CONFERENCE AT THE COMMAND HEADQUARTERS AT 11:00 A.M.

She didn't go—she was afraid for her life.

CHAPTER X
LONDON

When Joanna learned about the attempt on Aśka's life, she flew into a rage. Fixing Piotr with her cold, steely gaze, she strained the words from the depths of her throat.

"How could you let those bandits track her down? Do you realize how it could have ended?"

"Mom, it's not his fault. We don't even know who it was," Aśka interjected, defending Piotr.

"From today on, you'll have round-the-clock security. You won't even go to the *bathroom* without it until this is all cleared up."

"You're right, Joasia," Piotr conceded, his face grim. "Aśka shouldn't set foot outside the residence for the next two weeks. Meanwhile, I'm going to London to follow up on our latest leads."

Piotr pulled his nearly new suitcase from the hall closet and began to pack. He had an afternoon flight to London, where Aśka had booked him a room at The Dorchester.

"Why such a luxury?" he asked her.

"You need to impress everyone you meet. Invite them there, and they'll become more predictable and pliable before you even start talking."

Before he left, he made her promise not to leave Joanna's residence until he returned from London. She watched him get into the limousine for the airport, thinking this was their last chance to find her sister. After this, only agencies like ITAKA and TV appeals would remain.

At the airport, Piotr met the two counterintelligence officers he was bringing along. *They could be useful, and if not, it's a pleasant trip on my dime*, he thought, looking at the young, shapely woman, their latest recruit. Walking beside her was his lead officer, a specialist in eavesdropping techniques.

Upon arriving at the hotel, Piotr went to a friendly intelligence agency to inquire about the lawyer handling the case of Joanna's missing girls. They had cooperated on several cases involving two rapes and one particularly brutal murder. While the murder had been committed by a Pole on British soil, the two rapes were committed by Brits in Poland. All cases had been successful, and their mutual reputation had grown in value.

This time, Piotr faced a different problem. The case involved a lawyer from a small London agency that Joanna had used, which required cooperation with another investigative firm Piotr wasn't familiar with.

Maybe it's best to go to him and openly offer to buy the information. But it was a matter of trust. He couldn't trust Ronson's firm, which, paid by its client, might not disclose all the information it had obtained and, as he suspected, might even be working against him.

I need to have an ace up my sleeve before I approach him, he pondered.

He didn't know the market himself, and it would be easier for a friendly British agency to pressure Ronson, backed by irrefutable arguments. That leverage would be the illegal collection of material for DNA testing and its illicit use. In England, that's a crime. The catch was that Piotr didn't know how Attorney Ronson's firm had gotten hold of the material.

With slight apprehension, he entered the Director's office at the intelligence agency.

Tony Evans leaned back in his leather chair. He wasn't sure how to treat the unusual request from his Polish counterpart. In a dry tone, he advised him to approach Lawyer Ronson in person.

"I can't. There's a conflict of interest. I'm acting on behalf of the Head of DALCOM, and I'm personally involved."

The name DALCOM made a modest impression on him. He still didn't know what to make of Piotr.

"Don't be fooled by the Ronson Company's activities. Ronson personally acted against his client's interests, and by obtaining DNA comparison material, he committed a crime. He either didn't complete the task assigned to him, or he didn't want to disclose the information he obtained," Piotr explained to Evans. "Your job is to find out why. I should mention it wasn't a very complicated assignment."

Tony shifted uneasily. He was starting to dislike this; besides, Piotr's explanation of what he really wanted—"to get everything Ronson learned in Poland"—was quite cryptic. *What is this all about?*

"I'd have to act against another agency; it could be dangerous. I could lose my reputation if your suspicions turn out to be unfounded."

"I've prepared a report detailing the information I need you to obtain. It includes the data I have and the locations Ronson visited in Poland. I have no information on his contacts regarding this matter here in England. I have a strong feeling all the threads lead back to London."

Tony gave him an appreciative look. This is something concrete, not a wild goose chase.

"We'll look into this report, but I'm not promising anything," he finally said.

Piotr was furious internally; he wanted to stand up and tell this self-important Englishman, *Screw it, I'll handle it myself.* Instead, he said:

"Fine. I'll be waiting at The Dorchester for your findings."

Tony put down the golden pen he had been waving in front of Piotr's nose.

"The Dorchester, you say? Well, I'll see what I can do," he assured him in a friendlier tone.

That afternoon, when he called Joanna, he complained about the cold reception at the London agency.

"You know, Joasia, they think they're the center of the universe."

Hours later, while at lunch, he received an urgent call from the officer tracking "Zdzira."

"I'm at the Gdańsk airport. Zdzira has a ticket to London. They must have followed you and sent her after you."

He received this news with anxiety.

"Send me a photo of her on my phone. I'm sending my team to London Airport now. We'll see what brings her here."

He called Renia's room.

"You have a task—the subject is at the Airport. Pick up Kamil in two hours; I'm sending you a photo now. Don't lose her and report everything to me."

Within ten minutes, they set off for the airport in two cars. *The flight from Gdańsk to London today will be faster than driving from central London to the airport,* thought Piotr, worried if they would make it in time. He mentally thanked Aśka for her foresight; she was the one who had rented them three cars.

"They might come in handy," she had said, handing him the order before departure.

That morning, Joanna received a DHL delivery. Inside were the rest of the corals and a photo of the Senator and the "Bandit" with a van in the background. A navy-blue van. Everything was becoming clear.

Aśka faced a major problem. She was an expert at obtaining information, but she always needed a starting point—a name, a date of birth, or something similar. A PESEL or NIP number was ideal. That information was always on some official website. Once they used their computer to contact an office, they were like an open book to her.

The obstacle was the era before computers. From that time, only tedious and meticulous investigative work remained.

This time, Aśka quickly discovered the sender.

"It was easy," she told Joanna. "The shipment came from a DHL office, but the sender checked online for its status, so I tracked that computer. Within an hour, I cracked a simple, short password and had access to its contents." She transferred the data to her own computer and quickly saved his information on a separate disk.

"This is the company computer for the Lucky Restaurant. There's nothing special about it, but its contents might interest more than just the Tax Office." Speaking in a calm tone to Joanna, she could barely contain the excitement she felt after seeing the photos stored on it.

Joanna, listening to Aśka, sighed and put her arm around her.

"Piotr was right—Zdzira is involved. Now I'm going to deal with her."

Aśka decided to come out of hiding. She missed her boyfriend and the newsroom. She was no longer afraid. The Senator is dead, only the Bandit and Pikuś are left, and what about General Z...? They know about me, as shown by the email I got from the Colonel. But he has bigger problems to worry about, she thought.

She had been wanting to meet Henry for a long time; she hadn't seen her boyfriend in three days.

Taking advantage of Piotr's absence, she decided to play the next move in her own style. She got into her new Porsche—a gift from Joanna—and set off for Kościuszko Square.

Two cars and one motorcyclist, like inseparable shadows, followed her.

"Alpha One, overtake. I'm heading to the Square, take the lead," she said into the microphone. A Mercedes screeched past her and positioned itself about 50 meters ahead.

Seeing this, Aśka smiled to herself. *Now there's nothing to fear.*

She parked her car at the beginning of the square, in the parking lot next to a small bank that had been closed for some time. As she got out, she touched the holster of the small pistol hidden on her hip. This was the condition set by both Piotr and Joanna.

"Only with this and security can you leave the mansion."

She walked slowly to the other side of the pavement, heading towards her apartment. *They need time,* she thought about the bodyguards. She didn't want to make their job harder; she was a professional herself and knew what their work entailed. She entered the building. Her team leader's words sounded in her ears.

"Alpha here—don't go in there alone."

She didn't listen.

"Wait for us!" This time he shouted.

They ran across the street toward the gate where she had just disappeared. She entered the stairwell, where two burnt-out light bulbs left the corridor dark. The faint glow from the glass door made her squint, narrowing her field of vision.

Walking towards the elevator, she noticed Pikuś emerging from a side corridor. He had apparently been waiting for her, because upon seeing her, he pulled a sawn-off shotgun from the long bag he was carrying—a weapon that could blast her and the wall behind her to pieces. She realized she was in mortal danger. She reacted as she'd been trained: she didn't run or try to hide, but instead closed the distance by taking a step toward him. The time he lost pulling the weapon likely saved her life. She took a second step, now half a meter away from him. She heard the elevator door to her left open with a soft hum. Out of the corner of her eye, she saw an elderly woman from the third floor inside. His gaze also shifted toward the elevator. In that moment, she lunged at him, grabbed the end of the shotgun's barrel with her right hand, and jerked it upward. With her left, she tried to draw the pistol from her holster.

The bodyguards were a few meters from the gate when they heard the first shot. Then, a second.

His heart pounding with fear, the first bodyguard rushed inside. A cloud of dust from the shattered ceiling shrouded the corridor like a frosty morning fog over the Gdańsk Bay.

Without a second thought, he rushed towards the attacker, who was struggling with Aśka over the shotgun. The weapon fired again, blasting into the ceiling. The bodyguard grabbed Pikuś by the neck from behind and struck his temple with the butt of his pistol. The man's limp body slid onto the cold terrazzo floor of the hallway, his grip on the weapon finally releasing.

A terrified Aśka was still clutching the barrels of the shotgun with her right hand, her own pistol pointed shakily at the assailant with her left.

"It's okay, don't shoot," the second bodyguard said in a calm voice as he ran inside and saw Pikuś fall. She carefully handed him the weapon and looked toward the elevator. The elderly woman was lying on the floor, motionless. Holstering her pistol, Aśka stepped into the elevator. The woman lay slightly curled on her right side, her eyes open and magnified by the thick lenses of her glasses.

"A doctor, quickly!" she called out to the bodyguards.

The second bodyguard handcuffed the unconscious Pikuś and checked his pulse. He was alive, breathing.

"Is she hurt?" the first bodyguard asked.

"I don't know, I can't see a wound," Aśka replied.

The corridor began to fill with tenants frightened by the sound of gunshots.

"The police are here!" someone shouted. But one of the bodyguards was already on the phone with the police, informing them of the situation.

Aśka slowly climbed the stairs toward her apartment. At the door, she ran into Henry.

"What's going on?" he asked.

"Nothing, Pikuś just tried to kill me," she replied in a slightly trembling voice. A bodyguard stood behind her, scanning the area intently.

"Go inside the apartment and don't leave. I'll be at the door," he instructed her.

She gladly complied. She entered the living room and collapsed onto the sofa. Only now did the stress hit her.

"Get me a glass of cold water," she asked Henry. "Not a word to anyone," she said to Henry and the bodyguards an hour later, as they were leaving the apartment for the police station.

Joanna called Piotr. He didn't answer.

What the hell is going on? Why isn't he picking up?

An hour later, her cell phone rang with a tone that brought her immense relief.

"It's me, sorry, I had to turn it off."

"I received a DHL shipment—the rest of the corals and photos. I'm sending you copies now. Aśka tracked down who sent the package," she quickly began relaying the latest events.

"Zdzira," he interrupted her.

"Yes, you're right. I just don't understand what made her do it."

"But I do."

"What should I do?"

"Pack your bags and get to London as soon as possible."

Joanna suppressed her burst of enthusiasm and joy at his invitation—whatever the reason behind it might be.

He spoke for a long time, and she remained silent until he finished. Her face contorted in a grimace of bewilderment. Piotr had told her something that made her freeze.

"I'll take the next plane," she said in a tender voice, quickly adding, "I love you."

"Me too," she heard. "I'm waiting, and I won't do anything until you're here," he assured her.

"Great—I'll be there this evening," she said and hung up.

She remained calm, albeit only on the surface; inside, she felt a pressure, as if she had eaten something heavy. *It's just nerves*, she thought. Piotr's words had thrown her off balance. She knew he would never tell her something he wasn't one hundred percent sure about. She had felt like this only once before—when he had informed her about finding her daughter. She knew why he had gone to London, but the idea that Zdzira had followed him was completely incomprehensible. *What secrets could be behind this?* she wondered for a moment.

With a firm determination to face the problem, she drank a glass of white wine and grabbed her phone.

"Aśka, I'm going to Piotr's in London," she left a message in her mailbox. "Call me, it's urgent," she added before heading to her wardrobe.

Throughout the flight, she thought about what Piotr had told her.

"It's good to see you, Joasia," Piotr greeted her at the airport. "Zdzira is in a hotel near the Hilton. She's being watched by two of our officers."

"What is she doing here? Did she follow you? How did she know where and when you were flying?" she fired off questions.

"I don't know—she was probably having me followed, not personally, but maybe she hired someone. I think Bandzior is behind it; he visited her a few days earlier," he explained his theory.

Three hours earlier, he had swapped his room for a suite on the seventh floor. Joanna liked the large, spacious apartment with all its amenities.

"Freshen up, rest. I'll order dinner to the room," he said, taking the suitcases from the bellhop and slipping him a generous tip.

She shook her head.

"We'll go downstairs, eat in the restaurant, listen to some music, maybe dance a little. I hope you're done working for today."

She stripped down to her underwear, took his hand, and led him into the large bathroom with its oversized tub. Everything glittered in gold and white. Shedding the rest of her clothes, she turned on the tap and stepped in.

"Come on, you're going to massage my back," she said, turning toward him with a mysterious smile.

"I'm not sure that's a good idea; they could call me at any moment," he replied with an equally defiant smile.

But his actions contradicted his words. By the time he finished speaking, he was undressed and ready to get in the tub.

"Now, tell me the details."

She slowly turned toward him and handed him a glass of champagne.

The next morning, Piotr's phone hummed quietly.

"She's walking towards the bridge. She's alone," Renia said, sending him a picture of the walking Zdzira.

"Don't lose her," he said, looking at the phone screen.

Something's wrong here. If she had come for me, she'd be near the hotel by now, he thought.

"I'll be right there," he said and quickly left the room, heading for the elevator.

"Taxi, quickly!" he called to the doorman. A black cab pulled up in front of him.

One of the intelligence officers was waiting for him by the bridge. Piotr discreetly approached him.

"Where is the subject?" Piotr asked.

"In those houses. Renia is waiting in front of the entrance gate."

They walked quickly towards her. After crossing the bridge, a small street led to a row of houses in a compact block. Their car was parked next to one of them.

"Where is the subject?" Piotr asked Renia as he got inside.

"Opposite, the second entrance with the brown door."

"I'm going in," he told the officers. "If I'm not out in three minutes—come get me."

He took the three steps to the front door in one stride. He stood before it and glanced at the three name cards next to the doorbells. Two English surnames and one Polish one. First floor.

What is Zdzira's last name? He tried to remember. It came to him in an instant.

He rang the bell twice.

"Who's there?" he heard a voice ask in good English with a slight Slavic accent.

"From Attorney Ronson," he replied in Polish.

"Please," the voice said, sounding familiar.

Who could that be? He thought for a second, but when he heard the metallic sound of the lock unlatching, he opened the door. He entered a small corridor. A wide wooden staircase covered with a burgundy carpet invited him upward. He quickly ascended and stood before a door with frosted white glass featuring ornate patterns.

He knocked.

The door opened slowly, and he saw Aśka.

It stunned him.

"What are you doing here?" he managed to cough out.

"I don't know you. Who are you?" he heard in reply.

Zdzira emerged from behind her. She looked at Piotr with an equally astonished expression.

"Mom, do you know this man?"

"Yes," they heard Zdzira whisper softly.

"May I come in?" he asked, his initial shock beginning to subside.

The girl looked questioningly at Zdzira standing beside her.

"Let him in," Zdzira said in a resigned voice.

"You mistook me for someone else. My name is Beata," the girl said, moving away from the door.

Piotr stepped inside.

That evening, in the blue room of The Dorchester Hotel, a great celebration was underway.

Aśka had caught an early morning flight at Piotr's insistent request.

"Can Henryk fly with me?" she had asked Piotr when he called her right after leaving Zdzira's mysterious apartment.

"You know what I think, but it would be awkward to bring him to the meeting I'm inviting you to. It's best if he comes tomorrow morning, but you decide."

"And what happened?" she tried to get something out of Piotr.

"I can't say anything."

"I'm waiting," he added, and hung up.

When she entered their hotel suite at noon, he gave her time to unpack and then invited her to dinner.

As they sat down to an exquisite dinner in the grand blue banquet hall, their spirits were high. It was hard not to be impressed by the soft blue radiating from every direction. The walls and decorations harmonized with the white and silver tableware, and the blue hydrangeas on the table completed the picture. Their efforts had been a great success. Aśka proudly presented her second "bombshell" article, this time with all the available data on the people involved.

In the article, she revealed the mechanisms behind the rigged military tenders for equipment repairs in Afghanistan, naming those responsible. She spared no one—not General Z..., nor the late Senator G... She detailed the possible causes of the Hercules crash and how it might have been orchestrated. This had contributed to the arrest of an Air Force lieutenant accused of sabotage and damaging Hercules components.

"This is the first terrorist act in the Polish Army," the Military Prosecutor had thundered later, apparently trying to score points by attributing such a motive to Major Zenon K...'s actions.

Although Aśka had clearly written that, based on her information, it was a typical act of revenge—for a brother killed, for a mutilated friend, for the military authorities' neglect of the families of soldiers killed in Afghanistan, and for abandoning the physically and mentally crippled veterans of that strange war.

Joanna's money, connections, and resources had helped Skowronek and the Agent from the Repair Works feel safe and comfortable in one of her houses. They would stay there until the threat passed. Aśka also revealed the positive role played by her mysterious informant—Karolina, an aide to Senator G...

"May her tragic death in the Hercules crash not be in vain," the capital letters in her article glared from the page.

"I need to lighten the mood; I'm going shopping. Are you coming with me, Aśka?" asked Joanna.

"No, we have something to take care of now, but we'll be very happy to join you tomorrow," Aśka declared, looking pointedly at Piotr.

So Joanna called a friend, and they agreed to go shopping together.

"We need to talk," Piotr said to Joanna with a mysterious smile on his lips.

When they were settled comfortably on the soft sofa, he took her hand and, looking into her eyes, said,

"Don't be upset, but I have something to tell you."

"If you start like that, I'll get angry right away, so just get to the point," she fired back, knowing his penchant for legalistic preambles.

"I found your sister."

"How? Where?" she exclaimed in an excited voice.

"Here in London."

After draining her glass, she blurted out,

"Zdzira!"

He looked at her with admiration.

"Yes. Zdzira is her mother—her adoptive mother."

"Damn, how is that possible?"

"It was likely Bandzior's doing. He arranged it during the Communist era—I have photocopies of all the adoption documents."

"Where from?"

"From Attorney Ronson. He discovered it and hid it from you. Bandzior was blackmailing him, so he never revealed it to you. Under pressure from our friendly intelligence agency, he confessed to everything. It's better for him than a lawsuit. He committed numerous crimes in Poland regarding this case, and here in England. But we've come to an agreement; I won't press charges."

"Oh God, and Mom knows?"

"No, and that's the problem. How do you tell her that Zdzira has been acting as a mother to her daughter for all these years?"

"And how do you tell Beata that her adoptive mother is the cause of so much suffering for her real mother?" Aśka replied.

"I don't know. But that's not all. Beata—that's your sister's name—insisted she would only come to us if her mother was with her."

"Damn it! So now what? What is she like?" she asked, curious about her twin sister's appearance.

"You'll see, but be prepared for a shock."

"What are you talking about? A shock? In what sense? Do you have a picture of her?" she bombarded him with questions.

"Of course I do. But I won't show you. I won't deprive you of the surprise."

"What are you planning?" she asked, more calmly.

"What are *we* going to do?" he corrected her.

"It's a good thing I held back yesterday from exposing the escort agency run by Zdzira. It violates several penal codes, and the girls working there are held against their will and forced into prostitution. I discovered it on Zdzira's computer," she explained to him. "There are photos of the girls in compromising erotic situations. I think they were blackmailed with those and forced into prostitution."

"That's sad and complicates things even more," he nodded and ordered two more drinks.

"Are you sure she's my sister?" she asked, just to be certain.

"Yes, one hundred percent," he assured her, a cheerful look in his eyes.

She knew that look, so she let go of further questions.

"Here's what we'll do. I'll tell Joanna everything, and you convince Beata to come to Joanna by herself—okay?"

Piotr looked at her anxiously; he wasn't sure about assigning Aśka such a task. "It will be easier for you to tell Beata what kind of person her adoptive mother really is," he added.

"Did Beata know she was adopted?" Aśka asked.

"Yes, but only recently. Zdzira told her that her real parents died when she was a small child. She assured me she genuinely knew nothing about Beata's real parents. And strangely enough, I believe her," he added unexpectedly.

"After all these years, she wanted to make up for the evil she did to Joanna, so she sent those DHL packages. She admitted to sending those men. But they were only supposed to scare her, not rape her. And here, I don't know whether to believe her. The girl who was in the van was Pikuś's sister. She was the one who told Zdzira about the whole incident and gave her the photos that were sent to Joanna."

"Why?"

"She was dying, and her conscience was tormenting her. At least, that's how Zdzira tells it."

"Well, that's that," he finished his explanation and reached for the phone.

"Beata? It's Piotr. I'm sending a car for you. I'm waiting with your sister at The Dorchester."

"Yes, don't worry, it's just the two of us."

He dialed a second number.

"Renia, go pick up Beata and bring her to us at the bar downstairs."

Aśka was nervously sipping her drink.

"Don't be nervous, she'll be here in a few minutes," Piotr reassured her.

Aśka, staring at the entrance, waited for her sister, swallowing nervously until Piotr finally couldn't stand it.

"Is your throat dry? Here," he said, handing her a glass of water.

After fifteen minutes, she saw Renia coming down the stairs, and right behind her, she saw *herself*.

She stood up, excited. "That's me! We're even dressed similarly," the thought flashed through her mind.

Beata looked at Aśka in amazement. *It's impossible. I think there's a mirror there and my reflection in it.* But the figure in the mirror was walking towards her with outstretched arms.

Their mutual shouts of astonishment, followed by weeping and sobbing, mixed with joyful exclamations and bursts of nervous laughter, drew the attention of the entire room.

People began to applaud when Piotr announced loudly, in his own style, "You are witnessing the first meeting of these sisters after 28 years!"

If either of them had any lingering doubts about Piotr's assurances, they now vanished with their tears of joy.

They quickly moved to the suite, escaping the curious stares of the other guests. They made it just in time, as several reporters were already crowding the front entrance; apparently, one of the guests had tipped off the press.

In the middle of the huge living room, they talked more calmly. However, the conversation faltered whenever it strayed towards Zdzira—though they didn't use that nickname in front of Beata, she quickly noticed they disliked her adoptive mother.

When Joanna called to say she was on her way back, Beata stiffened and wanted to leave.

"Beata, why don't you want to see your real mother?" Aśka tried in vain to stop her.

"Forgive me, but this is all happening so fast. I'm not ready yet. Besides, we should wait for the DNA test—Piotr promised to have it done."

"Okay," Aśka relented, seeing how scared Beata was. "We'll meet in two days in Gdynia. You'll fly in, and I, your sister, will pick you up from the airport."

"I promise. I'll be there," Beata said as she left.

A sorrowful Piotr escorted her to the car.

"Beata, don't worry, everything will be fine. Joanna, your mother, is a wonderful person. She didn't know you were alive, and when she found out, she started looking for you immediately."

"But she abandoned me," Beata burst out, her voice full of anger. "And she hates my mom," she added.

"Why would you think that?"

"My mother told me... just this morning."

"No, it's not what you think."

"Then what is it?"

"I'll come to you later, and we'll talk properly."

"Alright, I'll be waiting."

Joanna returned to the hotel and found Piotr and Aśka visibly excited.

"Joasia, sit down. We have something important to tell you," Piotr began.

Aśka sat down next to her and took her hand.

Joanna sat, her hands clasped nervously, her face slightly pale. Their expressions made it clear the news was momentous—though she didn't yet know what it was.

"Can you guess why Zdzira came to London?" Aśka began.

"No, just tell me already. You know I don't like long introductions."

"She came because of her daughter, Beata."

"So what? I didn't know she had a daughter."

"But... she's my sister," Aśka blurted out.

"And your second daughter," Piotr interjected, sitting opposite her.

"What is this, some kind of soap opera?"

"You're right, it's unbelievable. I think Ronson found out a lot and figured out the rest. She *is* your daughter, and Aśka and I have no doubts about it."

"My God, how could this have happened?"

"Don't be upset. We've already spoken with Beata, and I've questioned Zdzira. Everything has been clarified. We also have the adoption documents and other evidence confirming Beata is your daughter. The lawyer you hired discovered it too, but Bandzior also found out he had located your daughter and blackmailed him, so he never told you."

"What does Bandzior have to do with this?"

"He was the one who arranged the adoption right at the hospital. We know where Beata stayed until she was four—with his sister. When his sister died, Bandzior gave her to Zdzira. I will say one thing: she was a good mother to her and kept Beata away from her dirty business. Your lawyer, while checking the documents at the hospital where you gave birth, went to Bandzior's sister's place. He stole the documents from there and kept them, which is why we didn't figure it out right away."

Joanna paced nervously around the room.

"She doesn't want to see me?" she finally managed to cough out the sentence that had been stuck in her throat like a ball of wool. The thought that her daughter, found after so many years, had been raised by the architect of her misfortunes was suffocating.

"That's not it. Zdzira confessed everything to Beata, but she claims she never wanted them to hurt you—just to scare you."

"Does she know who her father is?"

"No. Zdzira never told her. Bandzior forbade anyone from talking to Beata about it. She knows nothing about him. All she knew was that her real parents had died."

"Then why isn't she here?"

"Give her some time. We agreed we would all meet in two days in Poland, once I have the DNA results confirming our theory. But it's just a formality; it's not really necessary."

"How is it not necessary? Why do you say that? Do you have something else?"

"Yes."

"What is it?"

"Beata is Aśka's spitting image. They are as alike as mirror reflections. When I first saw her, I asked, 'Aśka, what are you doing here?'" Piotr burst out laughing at the memory.

"So what now?" Joanna asked. "Are we going back, or are we staying here?"

"We're going back, and quickly," Joanna decided.

Piotr, happy that he had finally managed to find Joanna's second daughter, strutted around proudly.

Everyone was waiting for Beata's arrival. Joanna locked herself in the bathroom, fighting a nervous stomach. Although she wanted to go to the airport, Piotr convinced her it would be better for them to meet at the residence.

"Let's not make a spectacle for the paparazzi. Why give them a photo opportunity? Besides, your daughter wouldn't want her picture in all the country's tabloids. Also, Beata is returning with Zdzira—it would be terrible if you met there. Maybe it's better to call her by her real name, Ela," he suggested. "Beata would be uncomfortable if we used that nickname in front of her."

Aśka went to the airport. Slightly nervous, she wandered around the terminal, thinking about what it would be like to have a twin sister. The plane landed on time, and a few minutes later, the sisters threw themselves into each other's arms.

A stunned Zdzira stood next to them, watching the sisters.

"I don't need to introduce you to my mom," Beata said, turning to Aśka.

"No, I know your mom from the photos."

"Mom! This is my sister."

"I can see that. If it weren't for the clothes, I wouldn't know which of you is my daughter," Zdzira said in a soft voice, filled with a great deal of love.

They escorted Zdzira to a taxi, and then, accompanied by their bodyguards, set off in Joanna's limousine towards the helipad. They finally felt safe returning home. They knew that while they were in London, the police had detained Bandzior, Major Dębiński, and several soldiers from the base in Afghanistan. The General didn't have time to face a court-martial, and Pikuś was already in custody.

Punctually at five o'clock, Joanna's helicopter delivered the long-awaited guest right to the doorstep of the residence.

As they stepped out of the helicopter, Aśka took Beata's hand, and they walked towards Joanna, who was waiting in the doorway.

"Piotr, they're like two peas in a pod," Joanna whispered to him, utterly astonished by the sight.

A timid Beata did not greet her as warmly as Aśka had when she first learned the truth about her mother. They moved a little stiffly into the dining room.

They sat down at the table. It was obvious Beata was nervous—the helicopter, the grand mansion, and Joanna's status were clearly overwhelming. The conversation was stilted, despite Piotr's best efforts. They soon moved to the living room, where the latest news was playing on the large TV screen. The news anchor was talking about a major success for the police and the military prosecutor's office. The broadcast showed a man in handcuffs being led from a house. Aśka commented on the sight with sadness in her voice.

"Do you know him?" Beata asked.

"No! Why should I?"

"That was probably our father," Aśka said, watching Bandzior disappear into the police car.

"What else are you hiding from me?" Beata asked, her astonishment plain.

"No, that's not true," Piotr interjected firmly, surprising everyone.

All eyes turned to him with unconcealed shock.

"He thought he was," Piotr continued. "Based on the documents and information from that time, it seemed he could be the one. Back then, there were no DNA tests to confirm it. But it is not true—he was not and is not your father," he repeated emphatically.

"Joanna's mother came to the same conclusion, which is why she wrote all those names and numbers in her diary. They are the places she visited and the children she met. She was looking for a resemblance to Joanna in them. Now I can finally tell you," he added with satisfaction, looking at both girls with a tenderness they had never seen in him before.

Surprised by his words, the sisters first glanced at each other, then at Joanna, and were about to bombard him with questions when his next move astonished them even more.

Piotr stood up and walked over to Joanna. He knelt before her, took a blue box from his pocket, and produced an engagement ring—a white gold band topped with a diamond set in a golden heart. Lifting it toward her, he asked in a soft, pleading voice,

"Will you be my wife?"

Joanna didn't hesitate for even a moment. Her initial shock instantly transformed into an expression of pure happiness.

"Yes! Yes!" she exclaimed. The man she loved had finally decided to do what she had been waiting for so long.

He couldn't have chosen a better moment. She was happy and joyful, surrounded by her newly found daughters. They stood with their arms around each other, kissing like a couple of teenagers.

After the congratulations, applause, and hugs from Beata and Aśka, they sat down again. Piotr opened a bottle of champagne and said in his mysterious tone,

"Do you remember when Aśka found herself, and we said all we were missing was our second daughter for Joanna and a sister for Aśka? I joked that my hair should be tested for DNA too."

They looked at him curiously.

"Well, I did it. Just now," he added.

A silence fell over the room.

"Let's drink to the happy reunion of the *whole* family," he said, emphasizing the word "whole." After they had all taken a sip, he took both girls' hands and announced joyfully,

"I am your father!"

All heads turned toward him. They stared in amazement. Joanna stood up abruptly and froze, her mouth agape as if she wanted to say something but was at a loss for words. Finally, a question escaped her lips with a thin whistle,

"Piotr, darling, how is that possible? Where is this coming from?"

He reached into the inside pocket of his jacket and pulled out a DNA test report.

"These are the results from the most reliable material for DNA testing—blood samples from Aśka, Beata, and me. I asked Beata for her blood for testing without explaining what it was really for."

"That's what you needed it for? I thought it was about me and Joanna," Beata said.

"That's what I wanted you to think, but it was about more than that. It was about me."

"I got the results this morning. My dear daughters..."